The Arachne Portal

THE ARACHNE PORTAL

JOAN MARIE VERBA

FTL Publications
Minneapolis, Minnesota

FTL Publications
P O Box 22693
Minneapolis, MN 55422-0693
www.ftlpublications.com
mail@ftlpublications.com

Printed in the United States of America

ISBN 978-1-936881-61-1

Previously published under the title Modern Surprises

List of Characters

Modern Surprises LLC staff:

Madeline Chang: owner of Modern Surprises LLC
Jay Ecklund: receptionist
Irene Williams: human resources officer
L. M. Yeager: security officer
Yolanda Brookings: financial officer
Vivian Davenport: fabric artist
Ginnie Mae Parsons: company mechanic
Athena Fairbanks: company engineer
Stephanie Morales: company physicist, principal designer of Arachne
Terry Thompson: robot wrangler
Nadia Siddiqui: company programmer
Jean Rosenthal: company pilot
Sumita Patel: company doctor
Brittany Knox: company psychiatrist
Daphne Hawthorne: company chemist
Zoe Moore: maintenance supervisor

Others:

Charles T. Vance: billionaire industrialist
Thelma and Ned Yeager: married couple in charge of the Yeager estate
Zach Yeager: in charge of livestock and ice cream production at the Yeager estate
Carol and Philip Yeager: musicians, L. M.'s parents
Harmony Yeager: L. M.'s sister
Andy Yeager: in charge of communications at the Yeager estate
Don Quist: Jay's friend and former boss
Alex: bartender/owner at Dry Cactus bar
Sam: owner of flower shop
Ramona and Luis Santana: owners of the horse ranch near the Modern Surprises headquarters

Chapter 1

As he drove to the job interview, Jay Ecklund took an inventory of himself, to be sure that he had done everything possible to make a positive impression. He had worn his best suit, shirt, and tie, all fresh from the cleaners. The leather shoes were fresh out of the box. His dishwater-blond hair had been parted sharply on the left side and combed. When he had checked himself in the mirror, he thought even his spit-and-polish military parents would have approved of his appearance.

Jay's car, an eight-year-old Valedictorian with over 100,000 miles on it, had been freshly washed. He hoped it would not pick up too much desert dust as he drove along the freeway. Few cars passed him this far out of town, but any breeze would blow sand across the road, and rain was rare enough so that it was seldom washed away.

He turned off the freeway to a two-lane paved road, and looked ahead to see it curve around a rock formation. Once around the bend, he saw two large buildings. Both had been constructed of local materials, and blended with the geological features behind them. One appeared to be separate from the rocks; the other seemed to extend right into the butte. He saw an LED-style billboard near the top of the butte displaying the company name: MODERN SURPRISES LLC. Jay presumed the building underneath the sign was company headquarters.

Movement from the edge of the rock cliff caught his eye. Out of the shadows he saw a large motorized contraption about two stories tall. The bottom half resembled a tank, with treads. The front of the upper half showed a transparent cab. The driver seemed very intent upon her steering, leaning forward toward the dash. Two women passengers sat in seats beside and behind her. As Jay drove nearer, the passengers waved at him. He hesitated before realizing that since he was the only other person in the area, they must be waving at him. He waved back, and they gestured even more enthusiastically.

Jay took his eyes away from the strange vehicle to find a place to park. When he got out of the car, he saw a roofed entrance with windows that went from floor to ceiling. He opened the door, stepped inside, and crossed to another door that had a window on the upper half.

Walking in, he saw a desk with a high ledge in front of it. A woman with gray hair, wearing half-glasses with thick black rims, sat behind it. Standing beside the desk he saw a woman wearing a skirted suit. She extended a hand. "You must be Jay Ecklund. I'm Madeline Chang."

He smiled and gripped her hand firmly in the handshake. "Pleased to meet you."

She turned and indicated the woman behind the desk. "This is Vivian Davenport, our fabric artist."

He reached over and shook her extended hand. "Jay Ecklund. Pleased to meet you."

"I hope you're hired," Vivian said. "I hate working the phones."

"As do we all." Madeline turned to Jay. "If you'll come with me to my office...?"

He followed her up an open spiral staircase to a large room. The windows overlooked the parking lot. She sat behind a huge mahogany desk, facing away from the windows. Jay glanced around and saw a large wooden cabinet to his left, with its doors closed. On the wall were certificates recognizing her as a notable businesswoman, framed pictures of her in a military uniform, and other pictures of her standing with famous scientists and public office holders.

She extended a hand to a chair in front of her desk. "Have a seat, Mr. Ecklund."

He sat in the chair. It was nice and bouncy and upholstered. Ergonomic, too. "Thank you."

A laptop on the desk was open but at an angle where he could not see the screen. She glanced at it. "I have read your résumé, Mr. Ecklund, and your cover letter." She turned to him. "I also had a glowing recommendation of you from Don Quist, who served with me in the Army."

Jay nodded. "He also recommended you to me, quite highly."

She smiled. "Don said he was sorry that you were laid off. I take it that the organization you worked for decided that a receptionist was unnecessary and the duties could be spread among the other employees?"

Jay nodded.

Her smile grew wider. "I think they'll find that was a mistake." She glanced back at the laptop. "I see that your degree is in communications, you've worked as a civilian at various military bases or for defense contractors."

"Yes, ma'am."

"You like working phones?"

"Oh yes, ma'am. I love phones. My parents said when I was a toddler I slept with my toy phone instead of a teddy bear. Worked as a 911 operator while I was in college."

"That must have been challenging."

"I like talking to people, and helping them. I loved the job."

"When you think of your ideal world, what comes to mind?"

Jay raised an eyebrow. He had never received an interview question like that before. "A world where people are kind to each other and everyone's basic needs are met."

She nodded. "What do you know about our company?"

He straightened in the chair. "It was established a couple of years ago. Don told me that you invent things and make a profit from the patents. I understand that you created the CarryAlong smartphone and the MovingMap GPS, for instance."

"That's right. We have a lot of creative people working here, and some of them are...idiosyncratic. Would that bother you?"

"No, ma'am. As long as people aren't hurting anything, it's all the same to me."

"Do you know how to use the QRS phone system?"

"Yes, ma'am. There isn't a phone system I don't know about."

"The salary for the job is...." She named a figure. "Is that acceptable to you?"

"Yes, ma'am."

"We also pay bonuses if you develop a product or do community service. If you do community work, just have a supervisor sign a slip indicating how many hours you worked."

"That sounds great."

"There's a 90-day probationary period, after which your record will be reviewed for a permanent hire."

He nodded. "That's fair enough."

"You get a housing allowance for that period, and afterwards, you are eligible, if you wish, to live in company housing, rent-free, next door. Each unit has two bedrooms, a full bath, kitchen, dining area, and living area."

"Wow," he muttered before thinking about it.

Madeline simply moved on. "You can also pick your own job title, within reason."

He smiled.

"If I hired you, when could you start?"

He spread his hands. "Anytime, ma'am."

"How about now?"

He swallowed. "You mean I'm hired?"

"Yes."

He stood, took her hand in both of his, and shook it. "Thank you, ma'am."

"You're welcome." She gestured at the seat with her free hand. "If you'll sit down again, I'll give you some basic information."

He let go of her hand and sat, smoothing his hair. "Yes, ma'am."

"We're all on a first-name basis here. But don't shorten anyone's name without their permission. For instance, Vivian doesn't take to being called 'Viv.'"

"Yes, ma... Madeline."

"Dress is fairly casual unless we have a distinguished guest or go to a public event, in which case we'll give you a day's notice. A knit or button-down shirt, dress jeans, and walking shoes in good condition are fine."

He nodded.

"We give you four weeks paid vacation, and four weeks paid sick leave, meaning we expect you to *stay home* if you're feeling ill."

He nodded.

"Because our research is proprietary until the date of product release, there are certain areas of the building you will not be admitted to until you pass the 90-day probationary period. Of course you'll hear discussion of projects under development during that time and you will be expected to keep them confidential. You'll be asked to sign a confidentiality agreement."

"I've worked on military installations before. I can keep a secret."

"Glad to hear it." She stood. "Let me introduce you to Irene Williams. She's our human resources officer. She'll show you around."

Madeline led Jay back down the stairs and behind the reception desk to an office with windows facing both outdoors and the building's interior. He recognized one of the women who had waved to him outside. She rose from her desk and walked to the door to meet them. Now that he was up close, he saw that she was an adult with Down syndrome, somewhat shorter than both he and Madeline, with black hair cut short.

"Irene, this is Jay Ecklund, our new receptionist. Would you show him around and have him fill in the personnel documents, please?"

Irene smiled. "Right away!" Madeline left; Irene turned to Jay. "I'll show you around first, and then we can come back here and fill out forms."

"Okay."

She started to lead him through the ground floor, pointing out the restroom locations as they walked. He noted they were all single-occupancy restrooms.

Vivian called to them from the reception desk. "Is he hired?"

Irene turned in her direction. "Yes, but I have to show him around first."

Vivian threw her arms up in the air. "Hooray!"

Irene passed a room with windows. In fact, all the offices seemed to have windows where one could look inside. This particular office had a lot of large tables with fabric on them, plus a couple of sewing machines and various other equipment. The door was open. "This is Vivian's office."

The next office, also with windows, was occupied by an African American woman wearing glasses with black rims— similar to the ones Vivian wore, but oval instead of split across the middle.

"Yolanda, this is Jay Ecklund. He's our new receptionist." She turned to Jay. "This is Yolanda Brookings. She's our financial officer. She signs the checks."

Yolanda stood and walked over, holding out a hand. "Among other things." She shook hands with Jay. "Pleased to meet you."

He nodded. "Pleased to meet you, too."

Irene gestured. "I'm showing him around."

"See you at the staff meeting." Yolanda returned to her desk.

Irene led him to a large room with several small tables and chairs. "This is our lunchroom. We ask people not to eat at their desks because it leaves crumbs. You can have a coffee or covered beverage container at your desk, though." She opened some cabinet doors. "Here's where the food and plates and utensils are. You can have your own cup, just put your name on it with a permanent marker. The food is free to employees. We mostly have pasta. Do you like pasta?"

"Oh, yes."

"Good. This is the refrigerator, the microwave, the toaster oven, the coffee maker, the hot water heater, and the dishwasher, where you can put your dishes and cups and utensils when you're done with them."

"Sounds good."

She led him to a closet just off the lunchroom and opened the door. There were shelves with bottles and tubes and various boxes. "This is where we keep the bandages and aspirin and such. If you're hurt at work, let Sumita—Dr. Patel—know."

"You have a doctor on site?"

"Yes, though you probably won't see much of her. She stays mostly in her lab doing research."

"I see."

"You'll meet just about everyone at the staff meeting tomorrow. You're supposed to be here at eight am and the staff meeting is at eight-thirty."

"I'll be here."

She led him to another office and peered in the door. The name plate said, "L. M. Yeager, Security." She turned back to Jay. "L. M. isn't here right now, but you'll probably see her tomorrow, too."

"What does 'L. M.' stand for?"

Irene smiled. "If she wants you to know, she'll tell you."

"Fair enough." He glanced inside the office. He could see a lot of angel figurines on the desk and the shelves and cabinets. Each was about three inches high. "I take it she collects figurines?"

"Oh, those are her angels. She makes them herself from wax. She has a mold." Irene reversed course and led him back to her office. In addition to her desk, there was a small table with a laptop on it and a chair behind it. She invited him to sit with a gesture. "These are the tax and other forms you have to fill out."

Jay sat. "Okay."

Irene sat back at her desk. "Just let me know when you're done with them."

He began to fill them out. "These are well organized."

"Nadia is a good programmer. You'll see her at the staff meeting."

When Jay was finished with the forms, Irene led him back to the reception area. "This is your desk."

Vivian stood from the chair and shook Jay's hand. "Thank you, thank you, thank you. Now I can get back to work." She put her headset in a box that had her name on it and hurried away as if expecting someone to catch her and push her back into the receptionist's chair.

Jay sat.

Irene reached into a box and brought out a headset in a clear wrapper. "These are sanitized every evening by our maintenance supervisor. Put your name on your own box. When you go to lunch or breaks, Vivian or I will take over for you." She gestured. "Those are our headsets."

Jay took out the headset and put it on. "Got it."

"Lunch for you is from eleven-thirty to twelve-thirty," Irene explained. "You can take a fifteen-minute break in the morning, and one in the afternoon. Quitting time is four to four-thirty." She indicated the computer on the desk. "If you're not working the phones, you're allowed to use the computer to read articles or do research. You're not allowed to play games, though."

Jay nodded. "That sounds fair."

Irene used the mouse to bring up a screen. "If someone calls, you can type in their question here and the computer will tell you who to direct the call to."

"That's impressive."

"Nadia is a good programmer." Irene brought up another screen. "Here's the company directory and contact information."

"Got it."

Irene indicated two large monitor screens, on opposite sides of the room, mounted near the ceiling. Each showed a weather channel. The sound was turned off, and the closed captioning was on.

"We use these to keep up with the news and weather. Vivian likes to watch the weather. You can change channels or bring up an internet site here," she indicated a console display, "or on the wall panel near the door intercom." She pointed.

"Can I switch to any channel?" he asked.

"You can, but there are only a dozen channels. Madeline doesn't want us watching the entertainment channels unless we're on break. And keep the sound off unless everyone wants to hear."

"I'll remember."

"If you have any other questions, let me know. I'll be in my office."

"Thanks." After Irene left, he began familiarizing himself with the system. The QRS protocol was sophisticated and top-of-the-line—one of his favorites to use, though most places he had worked did not go to the expense to get it. He explored the computer and found a number of company files, some of which asked for a password to open. The files without passwords he did open and examine, especially those describing the building wiring and telecommunications.

He had forwarded a couple of calls and was just about to ask Irene to relieve him for lunch when he saw a large robot rolling down the aisle toward him. The robot appeared to be a narrow post with a sphere on top. The sphere had long metal spikes sticking out of it.

Suddenly, beams of light issued from the spikes, going *ping! ping! ping!* off the walls and ceilings. Jay immediately dived under his desk. The sounds and lights reminded him of a ray gun fight in a science fiction movie.

"Turn that thing off!" Vivian shouted.

The noise stopped.

"Terry, this is not 'freak out the new guy' day," Madeline said.

Jay emerged from under the desk to see Vivian and Madeline standing near his desk. He also saw a tall figure standing by the robot, presumably Terry. Terry was thin, with a long narrow nose and short shaggy brown hair, dressed in a country-western outfit featuring an embroidered denim shirt, denim pants, and boots.

"Are you all right?" Madeline asked Jay.

"Yes."

"What are you trying to do, scare him off?" Vivian demanded.

"Sorry! I didn't know."

Madeline gestured. "Terry, this is Jay Ecklund, our new receptionist. Jay, this is Terry Thompson, our robot wrangler."

Jay reached out and shook Terry's hand. "That's an impressive robot."

"I'm *really* sorry."

"Don't worry about it," Jay said.

"Terry," Madeline said, "take the robot back to the lab."

Terry turned and pushed the robot away.

"You aren't going to quit, are you?" Vivian asked.

Jay chuckled. "No, Vivian, I'm not going to quit."

Vivian let out a sigh of relief. "Good." She returned to her office.

"You have good instincts," Madeline said.

Jay scratched his head. "Well, I'm a little embarrassed. I guess I should have known it was harmless."

"Don't apologize," Madeline said firmly. "You had no way of knowing and did the right thing to protect yourself." She gestured for Jay to sit, and when he did, she leaned toward a console on the desk. "As long as we're talking security, you've probably noticed the monitors here."

"Yes. One shows the entrance, one shows the parking lot, and one overlooks the road coming to the building."

"If you see any sign of trouble, press this button here. It's a silent alarm that goes to my office and our security officer's office. When in doubt, press it. I'd rather have a false alarm than miss a possible threat."

Jay nodded.

"This button right here raises transparent walls around your desk. The same material is in our outside windows. Bulletproof, and just about everything proof." She stepped closer to his chair. "Let me show you."

She pressed a button and panes of glass started to rise from the floor, encasing the desk. When they reached the ceiling, she pressed another button. "This puts them back." They retreated back into the floor.

"Good, I'll remember."

"I have monitors in my office, too, which show the entire building and surrounding areas. I'll alert you if I see something."

"Thanks."

"You'll meet our security officer tomorrow. She's out today." Madeline left.

Irene came over to relieve him. He went to the lunchroom and found a bowl of pre-made pasta in the refrigerator. He took off the wrapping and put it in the microwave. While it heated, he found a clean mug, used the marker on the counter to write his name on it, and poured himself some coffee. After checking to see that no one else was around, he drew a small pillbox out of his pocket, removed a pill, and downed it with a sip of coffee. Then he got a spoon and sat down to eat.

He still had time when he finished, so he walked out to his car, pulled his tablet out of its insulated box, grabbed his sun hat, and walked to a wooden lounge chair outside. Other employees sat at a nearby table with an umbrella over it, eating lunch. They waved at him and he waved back. Then he settled down to read.

After a few minutes, a woman wearing a faded blue jumpsuit sat in a similar wooden lounge chair next to him. She had a round freckled face and red hair. He realized this was the other woman who had waved at him this morning. She smiled and said, "I have an ereader too."

He extended a hand to her. "Jay Ecklund. I was just hired."

She reached over and shook it. "I heard. I'm Ginnie Mae Parsons. I'm the company mechanic. What are you reading?"

"Mystery novels. I enjoy trying to solve them before the detective character."

"I read romances. I don't read mysteries because usually someone dies, and that's sad."

"It is sad. That's why the detective works so hard to bring the killer to justice."

"Still, I'd rather read romances. There's a site on the web where someone posts all the romances that have happy endings and no deaths. I read those."

"It's great that the web has resources like that."

"I think so, too."

They both went back to reading.

The next day, Jay sat at his desk promptly at eight. At twenty-five after, Irene came over. "Time to go to the meeting."

Jay stood. "Who'll take over the phones?"

Irene leaned over and pressed a button on the console. "We'll just go to an automated message during the meeting. You can check it when we get back."

The meeting room was on the second floor. A large wooden table in a reverse-hourglass shape dominated the room. Irene sat in a chair near the bulge in the middle; Jay sat beside her. Others started to walk in: Terry Thompson, Vivian Davenport, Yolanda Brookings, Ginnie Mae Parsons. Another woman walked in and sat across from him. She was taller than he; she wore glasses with an orange tint, and held a toothpick between her teeth. Her denim shirt had L. M. YEAGER, SECURITY embroidered over the pocket. She reminded Jay of a kick-ass protagonist in a zombie apocalypse movie.

The room had three doors, all open. A woman entered through the door at his left. He estimated her height as four-foot-nine. Jay recognized her as the driver of the vehicle he saw the day before. Entering behind her was a woman wearing an olive green flight suit with JEAN embroidered over the chest pocket. They sat next to each other. A woman wearing jeans, a long-sleeved t-shirt, and a hijab came in and sat to the left of Irene. Madeline came in last, shutting the door behind her, and then shutting the other two doors before sitting at the head of the table. She held a folder. Once seated, she set it on the table and opened it.

Turning to L. M., Madeline said, "Lose the toothpick."

L. M. took out a small box, opened it, placed the toothpick inside it, and closed the top.

"First, let's welcome our new receptionist, Jay Ecklund."

Everyone, including Madeline, turned to him and applauded. Jay smiled and nodded.

"Jay," Madeline continued, "let me introduce the members of our team here that you haven't met yet. The others are in research or away on business." She turned to the woman in the olive green flight suit. "This is Jean Rosenthal, our company pilot."

Jay and Jean exchanged nods.

"This is our company engineer, Athena Fairbanks," Madeline said, indicating the woman who had driven the vehicle. "This is Nadia Siddiqui, our company programmer," she added, indicating the woman wearing the hijab. She turned to L. M. "This is our security officer. L. M. Yeager."

Jay exchanged a wave with each of them.

Madeline took a breath. "Now, down to business." She turned to Yolanda. "Yolanda has our financial report."

Yolanda looked around the room. "I'm happy to say that our robot kit is selling very well, and we have more than enough to fully fund Arachne."

Many of the others cheered.

Madeline turned to Jay. "You'll get filled in on that after the 90-day probation period."

Jay smiled and nodded. "Of course."

Yolanda faced Terry. "We know that Terry's latest creation works."

Terry leaned over in Jay's direction. "I didn't know you would be starting so soon."

Jay waved. "No problem." For the rest of the meeting, he just listened as the others went over the electronic and toy kits they manufactured or were in development. Jean and Athena talked about the company plane—apparently it was a new design and undergoing test flights. When the meeting adjourned, he followed Irene back to his desk.

Between calls, Jay spent his time continuing to get familiar with the company's communications capabilities. In addition to the office intercom, phone, and Wi-Fi systems, they apparently had their own satellites that could focus anywhere on earth, and a private encrypted frequency that could keep them in touch anywhere on the planet. They could also pick up frequencies from just about anywhere. Testing it out, he eavesdropped on radio broadcasts from Canberra, Mumbai, Nairobi, and Anchorage, among other places.

Near the end of the day, he looked up to see L. M. standing in front of his desk. Since she still wore the tinted glasses, he could not see her eyes. A toothpick dangled from her mouth. She carried what seemed to be a weapon. It resembled a large toy water gun, but instead of being made from flimsy plastic, this had a formidable metal casing.

Nothing was said for about half a minute. Thinking that some comment on his part was expected, Jay guessed, "Duck hunting season?" The nearest body of water was over 100 miles to the west, but it was all he could think of to say.

"Kill weeds!" she insisted.

Getting into the spirit of the conversation, he replied, "Fight with honor. Return triumphant!"

She nodded, turned, and left.

Jay watched her through the windows as she exited the building. He noticed Irene walking up to him.

"L. M. has these moods," Irene said. "Vivian calls them 'the vapors.' It's okay, though. She's only mean to bad people."

"That's what I'm counting on," Jay said.

Chapter 2

The next day, as Jay drove to work, his car stalled at a stop light. He started it and it ran again, only to stall again at the next light. Remembering that the list Irene gave him of company benefits included free car repair, he started it once more, got on the freeway, and willed it to reach the company's parking lot. As he slid the car into the parking space, he saw Athena and Ginnie Mae standing in front of the entrance, waiting. The car's engine died even before he took out the ignition key.

"We heard you coming as we were walking to work," Athena explained. "Hand me the key."

Jay did.

"We'll take good care of your car," Ginnie Mae promised.

"Thanks."

When he reached his desk, he found a small flowering cactus there, in a compact green pot.

Irene called from her office door. "I saw L. M. put it there when she came in. That means she wants to be friends."

"So do I." Jay picked up the pot and examined it closely. "This is very nice." He put it on the ledge so everyone could see it.

When lunch time neared, Jay wondered how his car was coming along. On the monitor, he saw a white car drive up. A blond woman climbed out and walked in.

"May I help you?" he asked as she stepped up to his desk.

"I'm Harmony Yeager. I'm in town for a couple of days and I'm meeting my sister for lunch."

"I'll call L. M. for you." After he completed the call, he added, "She'll be here in a moment."

"Does she go by her initials here? At home we just called her 'Lyr.' Short for 'Lyrical Melody.' Our parents are musicians."

"Oh? What do they play?"

"Violin."

"Do you play an instrument?"

"Yes, guitar. Lyr plays the harp, or she did. I haven't seen her in months...not since I took the job at M.I.T."

"What field?"

"Mathematics. I'm in town for a convention."

At that moment, L. M. arrived. She and her sister embraced. They left the building, got into Harmony's car, and drove off.

Jay was about to rise in his chair to go to lunch when Ginnie Mae and Athena walked in. Ginnie Mae handed him his keys.

"We cleaned the fuel injector that was causing the problem, changed all the fluids and filters, and did a complete tuneup," Ginnie Mae said proudly. "Good for another 100,000 miles."

"Thank you both," Jay said.

Ginnie Mae smiled and left.

Athena wore a stained coverall and wiped her hands on a rag. "Yes, the Valedictorian is a nice, sturdy car, built to last."

"Do you drive one?" he asked.

She smiled. "No, I only drive cars I design myself."

"Which ones have you designed?"

She raised her head, then counted on her fingers. "Let's see. I designed the Predator, the Firedrake, the Lancelot E-series—" She faced him. "Not the A-series—that was a pile of junk."

Jay nodded. "I know. My brother bought one."

"It appealed to a certain demographic. Passed all the safety tests, and sold enough to satisfy the auto executives. But it was still junk."

"Which one do you drive?"

"Oh, I drive the Airhawk. Customized mine, of course."

"Design any others?"

"No. We were going to present the Airhawk at the auto show when the production manager came up to me and suggested that I attend in a bikini and talk to the prospective buyers. I told him that since our marketing research showed that forty percent of our buyers were women, maybe he should show up in a Speedo."

"...and that's when they fired you."

"No, that's when they fired *him*. I quit. They pissed me off once too often. I wouldn't go back if they begged me— which, in fact, they did."

"Their loss, our gain."

She smiled. "Yes, best thing that ever happened to me." Stuffing the rag in a back pocket, she left.

Outside, he saw Harmony parking her car. L. M. got out and waved as Harmony drove off. When L. M. came in, Jay indicated the cactus. "Thank you. It's very nice."

"No problem!" L. M. insisted as she walked to her office.

At the end of the week, Jay sat in his usual spot at the Dry Cactus bar, nursing the one tall glass of beer that his doctor allowed him per week. The television near the ceiling showed the local baseball game; interested, he ordered a burger and fries and coffee and ate dinner while his team pulled ahead. He put cash on the payment slip and slid it to the bartender as he watched the screen.

"So, how's the new job?"

Jay turned to see Don slide in next to him. He pushed his empty plate away to make room for Don to put his beer down. "Great. Never a dull moment. Thanks for recommending them."

Don nodded.

"How are things at the old place?" Jay asked.

Don shook his head. "We've been scrambling to reorganize to make up for all the vacancies. I've been thinking of leaving and starting my own company."

"Good luck."

"Care to come with me?"

"You mean at your new company?"

"If I leave, yes."

Jay scratched his head. "No, I think I'll stay where I am. They have a fantastic communications system."

"You know, they're just a startup, and startups often fail within a couple of years."

"That could apply to you, too, you know."

Don threw his head back and finished his beer. "Touché."

"I honestly wish you the best, though."

Don nodded. "I know. Catch you next week." He left.

As Jay watched Don go, he saw Ginnie Mae come in. She spotted him and walked over.

"You left your credit card on your desk." She handed it to him.

He took out his wallet and checked his cards. "Oh, thanks. I made an online purchase during lunch and must have forgotten to put it back."

She nodded. "I didn't want you to think it was lost or stolen. I was coming into town to see a movie anyway and was going to stop at your apartment before, then I saw your car here."

The bartender leaned over. "Can I get you anything?" he said to Ginnie Mae.

"Just a Virgin Mary."

"Coming right up." The bartender turned away.

"What movie are you going to see?"

"The new romantic comedy."

Jay nodded.

The bartender slid a glass in Ginnie Mae's direction along with a slip of paper with the total. Ginnie Mae paid for the drink and told the bartender to keep the change.

Meanwhile, a loud noise from the television drew their attention. One of the players on the home team had hit a walk-off home run, ending the game.

Jay turned back to Ginnie Mae. "Do you like baseball?"

She took a sip of her drink and nodded. "I played it a lot with my brothers. One of them is in the minor leagues."

"Which team?"

"St. Paul Saints."

He nodded. "Good team. How many brothers do you have?"

"Six."

"Wow, are you the youngest, oldest, or somewhere in the middle?"

"Youngest."

A tall man approached Ginnie Mae. "This your boyfriend?" he asked.

"No," Ginnie Mae said. "We just work at the same place."

He smiled. "Would you like to come to my place? I have a 60-inch theater TV and I can pick up any baseball game in the world...major or minor league. We can probably find your brother live or in a rebroadcast."

She smiled back. "Thanks, but no thanks. I need to go now."

"At least let me escort you to your car, then."

"It's a motorcycle." She finished her drink and began to walk to the door.

The man followed. "Oh, a Harley?"

Ginnie Mae kept walking. "Custom. Friend of mine designed it."

Jay immediately thought of Athena.

Ginnie Mae stumbled before she reached the door. The man caught her and helped her up. Alarm bells rang in Jay's mind. He took Ginnie Mae's empty glass, sniffed it, took a strip of paper from his wallet and put it in the glass. When it turned color, he motioned to the bartender, then to the man. "Alex, that guy drugged the lady's drink."

Alex turned to the man, who almost had Ginnie Mae out the door. "Hey, you! I run a clean joint here! Don't ever come back here again or I call the police."

Meanwhile, Jay hurried to Ginnie Mae and pulled her away from the man. "I'm taking her home."

Before the man could respond, the bouncer got between Jay and the man. "Move along, mister."

The man left.

The bouncer escorted Jay and Ginnie Mae to Jay's car. Ginnie Mae mumbled incoherently as they got her into the passenger's seat and pulled the lap and shoulder harness around her. The bouncer went back into the bar and Jay walked to the driver's side.

Jay heard a noise and turned just in time to avoid the man's fist, which flew in front of his face. Enraged, Jay hit the man in his solar plexus with his elbow. The man crumpled to the parking lot's surface. Jay straddled him and punched him in the face. As he pulled his arm back, intending to pummel the guy, a voice in his head said, *The police will probably let you off if you just give a guy a black eye, but they'll slam you in jail if you put him in the hospital.* Jay kept his arm pulled back and forced himself to stand up and walk back to the car.

On the way to the company residence, Jay used the hands-free calling system to dial Madeline, who had given him her number in case of emergency. At the residence, he was surrounded by a group of women, some of whom took Ginnie Mae out of the car and got her inside.

Madeline, L. M., Athena, and Jean were left standing in the parking lot with Jay.

"So it begins," Jean said.

Madeline threw her an exasperated glance.

"Well, you don't think that was just coincidence, did you?" Jean insisted.

"No, I don't, but Jay, here, doesn't know what we're talking about."

"Oh. Sorry," Jean said.

Athena took a breath. "L. M. and I will go into town and get Ginnie Mae's motorcycle."

"You can probably call the cops on the guy...he's undoubtedly still there," Jay said.

"Oh, he's long gone," Madeline said.

Jay raised an eyebrow. "You're sure?"

L. M. momentarily took the toothpick out of her mouth. "Yup. We're sure." She and Athena walked toward a car and left. Jean went back to the residence.

Madeline put a hand on Jay's shoulder. "Come in with me for a moment?"

Jay nodded.

As they walked along, Madeline explained. "Ginnie Mae was raised in a loving family with a father and brothers who respected her and protected her. They all went out hunting, fishing, and camping together...as well as repairing the family cars, of course. She has a hard time wrapping her head around the fact that not all men wish her well." She stopped at a door and pressed on a panel next to it. The door opened; the lights went on when they stepped through. She turned right into a kitchen but gestured ahead. "Have a seat."

He walked into the living room and sat in a padded upholstered chair.

"What about a beer? I have Guinness."

"I'll take a rain check."

"How about coffee? Cappuccino?"

"Sure."

"Coming right up."

He heard whirring noises. Soon afterward, she came out with two steaming insulated coffee glasses. She handed him one and sat on a couch, placing her glass on a low table in front of her. "How did you know that her drink was drugged?"

"I carry test strips in my wallet and put one in her empty cup when she stumbled on her way out the door."

She picked up the coffee glass and sipped. "I take it you've been burned before if you carry test strips."

He took a long drink and put his glass on the table. "When I was just out of college, I went to a bar to celebrate my first paycheck from a new job. They paid in cash so I had a fat wallet which someone must have seen when I paid for my beer. Someone drugged my drink, led me out to the alley, robbed me, and beat me to a pulp. The bar staff found me when they locked up for the evening, and called an ambulance. I had a concussion and broken bones. Took me months to get back on my feet again, and I still feel some of the effects."

"Did they ever catch who did it?"

He reached down for the coffee and took another long drink. "Yes and no. There was a police investigation. They did get the surveillance tapes and ID'd the perp, who they saw putting the drugs in my beer. But there was nothing connecting him to the beating or robbery—no cameras in the alley—and I was too far gone to identify him myself. They brought him in for questioning, but all they could charge them with was some minor misdemeanor, and the D.A.'s office didn't think it was worth taking him to court."

"Sorry."

He lifted his head. "Well...the police said that a guy like him was bound to get into some other trouble sooner or later and land in jail. He had a long arrest record and had served prison time before he found me. Later, the police came to my apartment and told me that someone had beaten the guy pretty bad and asked where I was at a certain time. I told them I was at a baseball game, and showed them the dated receipt for the ticket I bought at the stadium. They said when the guy got out of the hospital he would be serving time because he had outstanding warrants and had skipped bail. He'd been hiding out at local gambling joints."

"Did the police ever follow up with you after that?"

"No. They sort of mumbled that they guessed the guy got what was coming to him, wished me luck, and left."

"Is the guy still in jail?"

He took another sip of coffee. "Oh, yes."

She looked at him sympathetically. "That's quite a story. I'm impressed you trusted me with it."

He faced her squarely and smiled. "How do you know I didn't make all that up?" He finished the glass. "Besides, the statute of limitations has expired by now."

The doorbell rang. "Excuse me," she said, and got up to answer it. He followed.

Two women stood in the hall. "Ginnie Mae will be fine," said one. "She'll sleep it off."

Madeline nodded. "Thank you." She glanced back, and seeing Jay behind her, continued, "You haven't met yet. Sumita, Brittany, this is Jay Ecklund, our new receptionist. Jay, this is Sumita Patel, our company doctor, and Brittany Knox, our company psychiatrist."

Jay stepped forward and shook their hands. "Pleased to meet you."

"Welcome aboard," Sumita said.

"Yeah. I've heard good things about you," Brittany added.

"Thank you." Jay nodded at Madeline. "I'll be running along now. Thanks for the coffee. See you Monday."

"Thanks again for your help," Madeline said, and the others added, "Yes, thanks!"

Monday morning, Jay arrived early and placed a small wrapped box on L. M.'s desk before she came in. Returning to his post, he hoped to greet Ginnie Mae when she came in, but she did not pass his desk. Consulting the electronic check-in feature, he saw that Ginnie Mae was on site. Either she used a side or back entrance, or she came in while he was in L. M.'s office.

At lunch, as Jay read his novel outside, Ginnie Mae came up to him.

He looked up and smiled. "How are you doing?"

"Fine," she said, though her expression was solemn. "Thanks for helping me."

He smiled. "Anytime."

She held up her own ereader. "Do you have any mystery novels where someone does something really bad and the detective gets him good?"

He sat up straighter. "Sure." He showed her his library and pointed out icons for appropriate titles.

She consulted her own ereader and downloaded two of them from her ebook provider. "Thanks," she said, and sat down on the next seat.

When his lunch break was over, he walked back to his desk and put his ereader away. L. M. came by, toothpick in mouth. She took it out. "Cinnamon."

"I thought you'd like it."

"Love it." She put the toothpick back in her mouth and walked on.

The first weeks seemed to go quickly. There were no further incidents. On a rare rainy day, Jay sat at his desk just after lunch. Irene had gone on her own lunch break. He heard singing. Looking up, he realized the songs were not coming from the overhead intercom. He checked his communications board. Nothing had locked on to a radio station. Perhaps someone had a portable radio in an office that they had left on. Neither Irene nor Yolanda nor Vivian was in her office, though. He stopped at the doors and realized the sound had not come from any of them. The selections were eclectic, representing a variety of musical styles.

Toward the end of Irene's break period, the singing stopped. Soon afterward, Irene, Yolanda, and Vivian walked in from the secure area.

"You're looking confused," Irene said as she passed by.

"I heard singing. Which radio station was that?"

Irene laughed delightedly. "That wasn't a radio station, that was us." Seeing Jay's puzzled expression, she added, "Sometimes we get together and sing during the lunch break...those of us who can sing, that is. L. M. acts as choral director."

Jay's mouth opened in an "oh," then smiled. "That was wonderful."

"It is. L. M. picks nice songs and tells us how to sing together better."

The bulk of the company's business was conducted electronically or by phone, so visitors were rare. Any movement on the monitor overlooking the highway, even a road runner crossing the asphalt, would capture Jay's attention immediately. More so when five black SUVs appeared, driving in single file.

Jay pressed the panic button and Madeline came into the area promptly. "Irene," she called, "go find Athena and tell her to get Stacy."

Irene ran.

Jay did not know who Stacy was—he thought he had met everyone by now—but hoped she could help with whatever was going on. He looked around for L. M. and realized he would feel a whole lot better if she were in the room.

Madeline leaned over toward Jay. "Put up the shield around your desk."

"What about you?" he asked, as he activated the controls.

"We'll be fine. We know what's going on. You don't."

Madeline stood aside as the panels went up around Jay. He could still see and hear what was going on around him. The cars steadily drew nearer. He turned around and saw that Yolanda and Vivian had left their offices and stood in the middle of the floor, looking out. He also saw, with relief, that L. M. had joined them. She did not seem to be armed with anything but the ever-present toothpick in her mouth. Terry walked up behind L. M. and stopped.

Meanwhile, the cars reached the parking lot. Four of them parked neatly between the lines. One stopped perpendicular to the lines in the middle of the lot.

A man emerged from the car nearest the front door. He wore dark sunglasses and a black coat over his black suit despite the heat. Three other men, wearing suits but no coats, got out of the same SUV and followed him.

"Lock the inner door," Madeline told Jay.

Jay obeyed.

They entered the outer door.

Madeline flipped on the wall intercom and spoke into it. "We don't allow visitors to carry guns in the building."

The lead man spread his hands. Jay got a better look at the suit under his coat: an expensive, tailored outfit that made the suits Jay got at the big box store appear shabby in comparison. He guessed that the man's coat and polished shoes were equally expensive.

"We have no guns," the man said innocently.

"Whatever you call them, they're weapons and you are not allowed to bring them in here," Madeline repeated.

The man brought out what looked to Jay to be a Glock and handed it to one of his escort. The three men left, removed items from their coats, and put them in the SUV before returning.

The lead man smiled. "We're here to do business."

"What sort of business?" Madeline asked.

"I wish to purchase the license and plans to Arachne," he said amiably.

"I have no information to give you on that. If that's what you came for, you may leave."

"Come now, I'll pay any price you name."

"We have no business to conduct. Good day."

"What would you say to a billion?" When he got no response, he continued. "Think of what you could do with that, what you could develop, what projects you could support, what charities you could donate to. You could do a lot of good with that."

"The answer's still 'no.' Good day."

"Perhaps if we had a meeting over lunch. Or coffee. Talked it over." He pulled at the inner door and found it stuck. Turning back to Madeline, he added, "Surely you aren't afraid of me."

"Not at all."

"Then why not let me in?"

"Because we have nothing to say to each other."

"I can be very persuasive...and persistent. I'm a man who gets what I want."

"You're not getting anything from here. Good day."

"Come now, don't make me use force."

Madeline turned to Jay. "Keep the shield up around you, but open the door," she said in a low voice.

"Are you sure?" he whispered.

She nodded. Jay released the door and heard a snick.

The man opened it and walked in. His associates gathered behind him. "I knew you would be reasonable."

Now that the man's voice was unfiltered, Jay found it pleasant, almost musical, despite the dangerous undertone.

"I opened the door only to make it clear to you that I'm not the least afraid of you and that you're getting nothing."

The man looked around pointedly. "You have quite a fortress here. Undoubtedly all of you feel quite safe. But what about your loved ones?"

"Mine are all active duty officers at Fort Liberty," Yolanda said. "Good luck getting past the missiles."

"I've spent thousands of dollars on private detectives trying to locate my relatives," Terry said. "If you find them, let me know."

"I'll pay you $50,000 to get rid of the whole blood-sucking bunch," Vivian said.

L. M. took the toothpick out of her mouth. "Every one of my family, except my sister, live in at the family's estate in Utah. The buildings are largely underground and rock-solid. Two of them are designated as emergency shelters for the county."

"What is that to me?"

"One of the family businesses is building demolition; another is fireworks. They blow up things for a living. So...I'll give you the GPS coordinates if you give me two days' notice." She put the toothpick back into her mouth and bit into it. "I'll sell tickets."

"...and what about your sister?" the man said.

"My sister is doing classified government work," L. M. said. "If you so much as appear on the horizon, you'll be getting a visit from the Navy SEALs."

He turned to Jay. "What about you?"

"Don't look at me," Jay said. "My family disowned me years ago."

He scrutinized Jay through the transparent partition. "I can see why, sitting like a sniveling coward behind a shield."

Jay laughed. "Quite the opposite. When I get really angry, or those who have my back are threatened, I'm a one-man wrecking crew. So you could say that I'm here for your protection."

"Pretty tough talk for someone behind a barrier. Why not come out and face me like a man?"

Jay grinned. "So says the one who has nothing to stand on. I've got the high ground and I intend to keep it."

The man turned to Madeline.

"Mine have Secret Service protection. You've got no leverage with me."

Throughout this conversation, Jay had an eye on the monitor. The same vehicle he saw on his first day had appeared around a bluff and rumbled toward the parking lot. This time, zooming in on it, he noticed that STACY was written on its side.

The man looked around the room. "You're all bluffing."

Yolanda walked over to the wall controls and changed the overhead monitor from the news channel to an internet connection. After typing in an address, she pointed. "That's my Mom and Dad, pictured right on the Army's website. My brother and sister are on other pages."

Terry followed suit, bringing up an internet news release. The headline read, STILL NO CLUES TO MISSING FAMILY AFTER SEVEN YEARS, LEGAL DEATHS DECLARED. She pointed and said, "Those are my relatives."

Madeline also brought up a news item: PRESIDENT'S DAUGHTER WEDS. She turned to the man. "See the groom? That's my brother."

L. M. accessed a website titled, "Tour the Yeager Family Underground Mansion." Below it were the tour days (Saturday and Sunday) and hours ("fireworks at dusk"), the ticket prices, plus announcements of concerts and ice cream socials ("freshly made from our free-range cows"). Jay also noticed a photo of a member of the Yeager family shaking hands with Utah's governor; the caption said the governor was congratulating them on their LEED certification.

Vivian's password was automatically masked, but her bank records account showed transfers to numerous parties. She jerked a thumb at the screen. "Rid me of those freeloaders and the next transfer is yours."

Within the booth, Jay synced his smartphone to the monitor. He bought up a video showing a stack of jack o'lanterns. Suddenly, the picture showed him with a bat smashing the pumpkins, and then for good measure, the potted plants next to them. He finished by kicking over the flower pot stands. "I didn't like the way they were smirking at me," he explained.

The man scowled.

Jay's attention was drawn to the outside monitor. STACY bore down on the SUV in the middle of the parking lot. The SUV doors all opened with a bang. Five men scrambled out and ran. Athena drove the two-story vehicle right over it. Jay heard loud crunching noises.

The man and his associates turned toward the cacophony. Madeline leaned toward Yolanda and whispered something. She nodded and walked off.

Those from the SUV pointed their guns at STACY and fired. The bullets ricocheted off STACY's side and pinged on the building's glass.

"Tell those men to stop!" the man told his associates. They ducked outside and shouted. The firing ceased. Athena drove STACY away, leaving behind a flattened vehicle.

The man turned back to Madeline. She took a slip of paper from Yolanda and handed it to him. "The amount reflects the purchase price of a new Lancelot A-series SUV."

Jay held back a smile. Athena had undoubtedly gotten satisfaction from flattening a piece of junk that had been advertised as "the toughest car on the road."

The man glared at Madeline, took the check, casually shredded it, and tossed the pieces over his shoulder.

"We're done here," Madeline said.

"For now," said the man, and turned.

"Forever," Madeline called after him.

He paused only an instant before walking out.

"Lock the doors behind them," Madeline said.

Jay obeyed.

"You can lower the shield now."

He did.

Vivian leaned over Jay's desk. "You aren't going to quit, are you?"

He laughed. "No, Vivian, I'm not going to quit."

"Good!"

Yolanda turned to Vivian. "I've been meaning to talk to you about all those money transfers."

"That's really none of your business, Yolanda."

"You're right, but did you know there are ways of helping your relatives without enabling them or bankrupting yourself?"

Vivian turned to Yolanda. "I'm interested."

They walked to Yolanda's office together.

When they were out of earshot, Jay turned to Madeline. "Was Vivian serious, or was she just calling their bluff?"

Madeline looked over to the office where the two women were talking. "Vivian has been known to speak without thinking about the consequences. She has a soft heart and doesn't have a mean bone in her body." She turned to Jay and smiled wryly. "You weren't thinking of collecting, were you?"

"Not me," he insisted. "My observation is that killing people causes more problems than it solves."

"Smart man. Get you far," L. M., apparently eavesdropping, remarked. She motioned to the screen. "About that display you showed them. That was really bad. Pathetic."

He cringed. "Uh, yeah, I know...."

L. M. motioned with her arm. "You gotta swing your arm this way, not that way, to put the most force in your smash."

All Jay could say was, "I'll keep that in mind."

Madeline turned to L. M., then Jay. "Now that the demonstration is over..." She tapped a finger on Jay's desk. "... go ahead and open the doors when they've gone." She walked toward the staircase, but as she passed L. M., she added, "Tell your Uncle Zach we're almost out of ice cream at the residence and we're ordering more. Have Yolanda send an electronic payment."

"Got it," L. M. said.

Jean appeared from the research area, holding the large weapon Jay had seen L. M. carrying earlier.

"You missed it," Terry said as she passed her.

"I didn't think they'd give up so easily," Jean said.

"They haven't," Madeline said. "We won this round, that's all."

"Yeah, they're too stupid to give up," L. M. said.

"What do we do when they come back?" Jean asked.

"The same as we did this time. We say 'no.'" Madeline walked up the stairs.

The others disappeared into the research area, except L. M., who lingered, staring out into the parking lot. Jay turned his attention there, where the men had pulled out a collapsible trailer from a surviving SUV and assembled it. They winched up the flattened SUV, then got into their cars and took off, trailer in tow.

"Athena took out the van with the surveillance equipment very nicely," L. M. remarked.

"They were scanning us?" Jay asked.

"Tried to, anyway," L. M. said, and walked to the stairway entrance.

Irene appeared behind Jay, beaming. "That was fun! Did you see?"

He smiled back. "I sure did."

Chapter 3

On the day his 90-day probational period ended, Jay got up and put on his best shirt and pants, and made sure his black canvas shoes were clean. He drove to work full of anticipation. Today he would find out the company secrets—or be let go. But he doubted he would asked to leave, if nothing else than because Vivian had repeatedly threatened to quit if he left.

Soon after he got to work, he and the others were summoned to a staff meeting. A cardboard box had been placed in the middle of the table. Most of the employees were there. When Madeline came in, she gave L. M. a look—she had forgotten to take the toothpick out of her mouth again.

When they were all seated, Madeline turned to Jay. "Well, Jay, what do you think? Are you willing to stick with us?"

He smiled. "If you'll have me."

"We certainly will!" Vivian exclaimed.

"I won't keep you in suspense, then," Madeline said. "Your performance record is excellent. I and the rest of the group want you here. So," she reached over and removed the top of the box. "Welcome to the company."

The others applauded and cheered.

Jay leaned over to see a cake which had "Welcome, Jay" inscribed on the top in icing. Zoe Moore, who he seldom saw because she worked evenings maintaining the building, brought plates, forks, and napkins. She cut the cake and served it to the others. L. M. distributed coffee mugs and poured from a carafe.

"Thank you, all," Jay said after he swallowed the first bite of chocolate cake.

"Now we can show you all the company confidential material," Madeline said.

"Yeah, and then we have to kill you," L. M. said.

Madeline threw her another look as Jay and the others laughed.

After the cake and coffee were gone, Madeline and L. M. escorted Jay to the security entrance.

"Give me your thumb," L. M. said, and held out a hand.

Jay hesitated. "Uh...."

L. M. grinned. "Don't worry, I'll give it back."

"It's to record your thumbprint so you can press it on the panel and get in," Madeline explained.

"Besides, we did a background check when you applied and we already know about your seedy past," L. M. said. "Cloning phones, getting free satellite TV...."

"That was when I was a teenager," Jay explained.

"And I bet you're even better at it now!" L. M. said enthusiastically.

Madeline sighed. "You're having a serious case of the vapors today, aren't you, L. M.?"

Jay chuckled and extended his hand. L. M. pressed his thumb against the red translucent panel. She punched some buttons on a keypad at the side. She motioned to the panel. "All right, Jay, press your thumb there and open the door for us."

He did. The large metal door slid to one side.

Madeline led them down a ramp to a large, dimly-lit area. As Jay's eyes adjusted, he could see that they were descending to the floor of an enormous cavern. The stone ceiling loomed high above them. What light there was seemed to be artificial lights from strategically placed LEDs. The air seemed fresh despite the enclosure.

When they reached the floor, Stephanie Morales, the company physicist, stomped toward them. She wore a thick exoskeleton. When she halted near them, she said, "Come to show Jay what Arachne is?"

"Yep," L. M. said.

Jay turned toward her and saw she had a toothpick in her mouth again.

The women led him to a low metal fence. It was so low he could have easily stepped over it.

"That's so we don't enter accidentally," Stephanie explained.

Jay saw what appeared to be a huge metal doorframe without a door. The top nearly reached to the ceiling, and the width was sufficient for a two-lane highway to pass through. He turned his head to one side. "It seems to be humming."

"B-flat," L. M. remarked.

He turned to her. "Perfect pitch?"

She smiled. "It's a gift."

He turned to Madeline and Stephanie. "Is it dangerous?"

"We don't know yet," Madeline said.

"It compresses space," Stephanie explained. "If we succeed, we should be able to step through this and end up anywhere we want."

"We're just testing it at the moment," Madeline said.

L. M. reached over to a small table Jay had not noticed before and picked up what appeared to be a clay discus. "These have GPS. We throw them through and see where they land. Right now it's tuned to my family's estate in Utah. Aunt Thelma and Uncle Ned look out for them when they walk the perimeter morning and evening."

"So far we're getting them exactly where we aim them, and the ones returned to us don't show any damage," Stephanie said.

"How do you give it a destination?" Jay asked.

Stephanie pointed to a control panel across the floor where Nadia sat. She saw the motion and waved. "Nadia and I program a multi-part code which the mechanism reads as a three-dimensional coordinate."

"You engineered this?" Jay asked.

"I did the original design," Stephanie said. "Then Athena, Terry, and Ginnie Mae suggested refinements and helped to build it. Nadia and I collaborated on how to operate it. It started out small scale; what we were hoping for was a way to compress matter so we could make better nanocircuits. Only it didn't compress...it moved what we put into it elsewhere." She nodded to the doorframe. "Eventually we constructed this full-scale model."

He looked up at it again. "And this is what our mysterious visitor was after."

"Yes," Madeline said. "Mr. Charles T. Vance isn't satisfied with having bought industries and governments. He wants power, and he thinks with this he can get ultimate power."

"So that was his representative we talked to," Jay said.

The women looked from one to the other. "No, that was him," Madeline said.

Jay opened his mouth, closed it, and opened it again. "But... I've seen him on the news. That wasn't Charles Vance."

"It was," Madeline said. "He was speaking through a simulacrum."

"An artificial person?" Jay said. "An android?"

"No, not an android," Stephanie said. "It's essentially a robot frame covered with a special clay, remotely controlled."

"Terry made the prototype," Madeline said, "and I'm sorry to say that we sold the design to him. We needed the money."

"He also happened to glance at a mind map I wrote about Arachne when he was in the building making the deal for the simulacrums," Stephanie said. "That's how he knows about it."

"Ain't making that mistake again," L. M. said.

"Were all the guys from the SUVs simulacrums?" Jay asked.

"No, just the one we talked to," Madeline said.

"How can you tell?" he asked.

"The eyes, mostly," Madeline said. "They look dead. That's why he wore sunglasses. But there are also subtleties in movement that you notice if you're used to seeing a simulacrum, as we are."

Jay turned back to Arachne. "What are you going to use it for?"

Madeline took a breath. "Rescue, we hope."

"How would that work?" he asked.

"Say a perp is holding hostages in a bank," L. M. said. "We just reach through and grab the perp. Perp'll never see us coming."

Sumita walked up to them. "We have to be sure it's safe for humans, first."

"It's still in the testing phase," Madeline said.

"The grasshoppers we sent through came back OK," Sumita said, "and the frogs. We have to send a mammal through, next, if we can convince Terry to let us use Widget."

"Widget?" he asked.

"Hamster," L. M. explained.

"We bought the hamster specifically to send through Arachne, but Terry seems to have become attached to it," Sumita said.

"She didn't object to the grasshoppers and frogs," L. M. said.

"Yes, but she never saw the grasshoppers and frogs before we sent then through. Widget's been in my lab for some time now," Sumita said. "I promised I wouldn't dissect Widget to be sure there was no tissue damage, and just use the MRI."

Madeline crossed her arms in front of her. "Well, when we're ready, Widget is going through whether she likes it or not."

"Why not just buy another hamster?" Jay said.

Sumita shook her head. "Same problem...Terry would see it as another adorable little animal."

"Well, fortunately, we don't have to make the test right now." Madeline turned to Jay. "We can take you through the residence and you can pick out whatever apartment you want from the vacant ones."

"That's very generous of you," Jay said, "but I like where I am now."

"You sure?" L. M. said. "Free rent, and you can take what you want from the common larder at no charge. Saves on groceries."

"It's private, if that's what you're worried about," Madeline said. "The walls are soundproof and no one's going to mind if you have a overnight guest."

"As long as I've done a background check and got a fingerprint," L. M. added. "Otherwise you have to meet your guest outside."

Jay shook his head. "It's not that. It's just that I like city living where I'm near everything."

"It's not that far away," L. M. said.

"Jay, remember what happened to Ginnie Mae?" Madeline said. "Now that you're officially part of the team, you may be a target. Staying with the rest of us is safer."

"I know how to take care of myself," Jay said.

Madeline exchanged a look with L. M. and turned back to Jay. "Well, could we convince you to at least name us as people to be notified in case of an emergency? That way we'd know if you are in trouble."

"That's not a problem. I don't have any family to list anyway," Jay said.

Don joined Jay the next time Jay was at the Dry Cactus bar.

"So," Don said as Alex, the bartender, put down the drink he ordered, "your 90-day probationary period is over. I presume you're still there."

Jay took another sip of his beer. "Yup."

Don smiled. "You must like working there."

Jay put the beer down and glared at him. "And just what does that mean?"

Don held up a hand, palm out. "Hey, buddy, just glad you have a job that you enjoy."

Jay blew out an exasperated breath as he took another sip of beer.

"I take it you know all the company secrets by now."

Jay turned to him and looked him in the eye. "You know I signed a confidentiality agreement."

Don shook his head. "Not asking you to tell me any. Just making an observation."

"Just making an observation about what?" Jay demanded. "What exactly are you getting at, anyway?"

"Nothing. Just having a conversation."

Jay stood and made a beckoning gesture. "Come on. Out with it. I know you're up to something."

"Up to what?"

Jay grimaced. "Stop with the bullshit innocent act."

Don got out of his chair and faced him. "Look, let's not let things get out of hand, here."

Jay nodded. "Yeah. Not let things get out of hand."

Don inclined his head and started to get back into his seat.

Jay threw a punch. It did not land, however; Don blocked it and put him in a headlock. Jay struggled as he remembered Don's military training and college wrestling experience.

"What's going on here?" Alex demanded.

"Call 9-1-1," Don shouted as Jay struggled to get out of his grip.

* * *

Jay stared helplessly at the ceiling in the emergency room and tried to remember how he got there. The Valium had kicked in and all he could do was lie there, slack-jawed. The curtains had been drawn around him so that he could not see beyond the immediate area. His wrists and ankles had been tied down, limiting his movement, even if he had the will to move, which he had not. Someone had covered him with a blanket. He was glad of it; the air conditioning had been turned up much too high.

He heard women's voices talking softly. One of them, at least, sounded insistent despite the low tone. Soon, the curtains parted. Sumita and Brittany walked in. Sumita stood even with his head; Brittany lingered behind her.

"I know you can't do much, after having been tasered and then injected with Valium, but if you can hear me, can you give some sign?"

"Yeah," Jay managed to say. His voice sounded much lower than usual.

"Can you understand what I'm saying?"

"Yeah."

She put a hand on his forearm. It felt good. "Let me bring you up to date. We got a call that you had tried to start a fight at a bar and the police were called. One of them tasered you when you tried to kick him. The paramedics gave you Valium and brought you here, where they looked up your record and called us. The bar isn't pressing charges, but the doctors here want to put you into an in-patient psychiatric unit."

"Naah."

Sumita smiled. "That's what I said, though not as succinctly."

"We're going to get you out of here, Jay," Brittany said. "Just hang on."

"Yeah."

The two women walked to the other side of the bed and looked at a computer screen. "Okay," Sumita said. "It looks like your medication was prescribed by Dr. McIntyre. The staff tried to contact her and found out she's in New Zealand right now."

"Not a coincidence," Brittany said.

"I bet it took a lot of trial and error before you got exactly the right medication to keep you on an even keel," Sumita said.

"Yeah."

"Someone did something nasty to you," Brittany said. "Our best guess is that the someone let themselves into your apartment and replaced your medication with sugar pills. They gave me your bottle when I came in and I had a taste."

Jay managed to form his lips and tongue to let out a raspberry.

"I agree," Brittany said sympathetically.

"Brittany," Sumita said. "Go to the hospital pharmacy and write a prescription for Jay's pills. Also get a syringe of the liquid form."

"How do we know they haven't tampered with the hospital pharmacy?"

"With current regulations on controlled substances tight as they are, I doubt it. Besides, why bother? They probably thought all they had to do was get Jay written up and incarcerated, one way or the other. But we'll have Daphne run an analysis when we get back, just to be sure."

Jay remembered that Daphne Hawthorne was the company chemist. He had only met her once, and that briefly.

Brittany left; Sumita walked back to where Jay could see her better. "We drove in with the van, and we have a stretcher. We'll sign you out and get going as soon as we can."

Brittany came back and gave Jay an injection of his current medication. She showed him a bottle of pills before pocketing them.

The two women left. Again, there were voices. He could make out Sumita's and Brittany's voices, but not the others.

"He is our patient," Sumita insisted, "and it says he's under our care on his medical record, even if Dr. McIntyre is listed as the primary. I'm an M. D. with privileges here, even if I don't use them often, and Dr. Knox is a practicing psychiatrist. Since the patient has already signed forms giving us medical power of attorney, we have every right to sign him out."

He heard reluctant mumbling, then footsteps walking away. Soon, Sumita and Brittany came back with orderlies, and somehow he was brought outside to a van. They carefully loaded him in the back. Brittany sat beside him as the driver—Sumita, presumably—started the engine. He fell asleep.

* * *

Harp music awakened him. Had he died and gone to heaven? He opened his eyes and saw he was in a room with cream-colored walls and a large window that overlooked the desert. Not heaven, then. Patting himself, he saw he was still clothed, but covered with a blanket and on a bed.

Gingerly, he sat up. He put a hand on his forehead. If all he had was a dull headache, he guessed he was lucky. With a hand on the bed to steady himself, he got to his feet. Looking down, he saw he still had socks on and wondered where his shoes were. Oh, next to the bed. He decided not to put them on, and walked around the bed, feeling stronger and more balanced as he did so.

He opened the door, walked down a short corridor, and gazed into a living room with sparse furniture: a table, a couch, a chair, a lamp. In the middle sat L. M., toothpick in mouth, playing a harp. She stopped and grinned when she saw Jay.

"'Music hath charms to soothe the savage breast,'" she quoted.

Jay smiled and nodded.

Sumita emerged from another room and handed him a glass of orange juice. "Here."

He took it and drank it.

She took the empty glass back from him. "How do you feel?"

"A little washed out. A slight headache."

"We'll get you some aspirin." She gestured. "Come with me and we'll make you breakfast."

She led him through a kitchen—where Brittany stood, wearing an apron, in front of a stove—and into the adjacent dining room where she eased him into a chair.

"What'll you have?" Brittany called.

Jay gathered his wits. "Uh...toast..."

"Plain or whole wheat?"

"Plain."

"Buttered?"

Jay nodded. "Eggs..."

"Over easy?"

"Sunny side up. And bacon."

"Coming right up." She reached for ingredients. "I worked as a short order cook in a campus diner when I was in college."

"Coffee...."

"No coffee," Sumita said gently. "At least not until you're stable again. No beer until then, either. Milk if you can drink it. Juice, water...."

"Milk will be fine. Or orange juice."

"We'll get you both," Brittany said. "Whole milk?"

"Got 2 per cent?"

"Sure."

Sumita put his bottle of pills and a bottle of aspirin on the table near him. "Daphne checked your medication and the residue from the syringe and they're what they're supposed to be. Take your usual dose after breakfast."

"I know."

"Sorry."

"No problem."

The three women joined him as he ate, though they just had juice or milk.

"Whose apartment is this?" he asked.

"No one's," Brittany said.

"Yours, if you want it," L. M. said.

"We just brought in enough food so we all could have breakfast, which we did before you were up," Sumita said.

"Did you stay here all night?" he asked.

"Sumita and I did," Brittany said. "We pulled out the bed from the couch."

He nodded. "Thanks."

"Happy to help," Brittany said. She and Sumita started gathering the plates and utensils and went into the kitchen.

"I'm going to get the asshole who did this," Jay said.

L. M. looked at him sharply. She stood, pulled over a chair next to him, and put a stockinged foot on it. Placing her forearms on her thigh, she loomed over him. "Listen to me, sonny. I was a police officer for eight years, and let me tell you, revenge is a waste of time. Most of the misery in his world is caused by people trying to get back at each other for one thing or another. It never stops until someone is grown-up enough to take the hurt without hitting back. That doesn't mean you have to be a pushover. But life, or nature, or karma, or whatever you want to call it, catches up with everybody and does a much better job at it than we mere mortals can." She shifted her weight. "Now Charles is building a house of cards, and sooner or later it's going to fall right on top of him. You'll see...and all we have to do is sit back and watch and laugh."

Jay was impressed that L. M. had spoken more than a handful of sentences at a time. He had not thought it possible that she could give a speech. "Well, I'm not going to be a pushover."

L. M. straightened up and put her foot back on the floor. "Not saying you have to be."

"And don't call me sonny," he added with a smile.

She reached for her toothpick and put it back into her mouth. "Got it." She nodded.

The doorbell rang. Before Brittany or Sumita could answer it, Madeline came in. She spotted Jay, walked over, and took a chair next to him. "How are you feeling, Jay?"

"Much better than last night."

"Good. Just take it easy for a few days. Don't plan on coming back to work until Sumita clears you."

He glanced toward Sumita, who smiled at him.

Madeline folded her hands on the table. "Jay, I strongly recommend that you move into the residence here. Today would not be too soon."

"Yes, I'm coming to that conclusion myself."

"We'll help you move, of course," Madeline said.

Jay nodded. "Do you have a unit that doesn't have cream-colored walls?"

Madeline smiled. "You can have any color you want. I'll send Vivian in to consult on design. Is this place all right, or did you want one with another view?"

"No, this is just fine, thanks."

She held out a hand. "Can you give me your apartment keys so we can get started?"

"I'd like to come along and supervise, if it's all the same to you."

Madeline looked over to Sumita, who nodded.

"We'll get together the vans and boxes," Sumita said, and ushered Brittany and L. M. out in front of her.

"I'll get Vivian," Madeline said when they had gone.

"Uh...before you go, can I ask a personal question?" Jay asked.

"Yes, though I may not give an answer if it's too personal."

"Okay. I wondered if L. M. had to leave the force due to her 'vapors.'"

"Well...they let her quit honorably before they fired her. She was a good officer, had citations for valor, but her moodiness just caught up with her. If it had been just one or two incidents, I think they would have overlooked it, but it got so that the others on the force didn't want to work with her, even though they did like her."

"I see."

"She goes back for police officers' picnics every year or so. They seem to be more cordial now that she isn't a daily presence."

"Yes, I can see how that could happen."

"Can I ask you a personal question?"

"Sure, if I have the option of not answering."

"Fair enough. Did your family disown you because of your disorder?"

Jay looked down at the table. "Yeah, they did. My mom and dad said *they* were *in combat* and *they* were injured and *they* didn't go on rages. They said I should just suck it up and pick myself up by my bootstraps. They didn't go for the medication thing at all. The rest of the family felt the same way...that I could just pull myself together if I really tried, and I wasn't really trying."

"That's surprising. When I was in the Army, most of my comrades were sympathetic to those who had PSTD and related issues."

"Oh, my family was entirely sympathetic to their military colleagues...but not to their own offspring, who had never had a whiff of combat."

Madeline sighed. "Sorry. Must have been tough."

He looked up at her. "It was. My friends picked up the slack, and most supported me, but it's still hard when your own family rejects you."

Madeline put a hand over his forearm. "Well, you have a family here."

Jay smiled. "Thanks."

Madeline left, and Jay cleaned up. He had just stepped out of the bathroom when there was a knock at the door. He answered it and found Vivian standing there with a laptop. "Madeline said you're coming to stay here. Good."

Jay motioned her to come in. "Somehow I knew you would approve."

They sat at a table. Vivian put the laptop between them so they could both see the screen. "If you want the walls a plain color, we can just paint the walls, but I can run off any kind of wall panel on the machine in the plant. We have a lot of designs...." She pointed at the screen, which showed a variety of squares showing various scenes. "This one's a moonscape. Stephanie has that in her apartment. This is a forest. Ginnie Mae has that one."

As she spoke, Jay examined the screen closely. He pointed to one of the squares. "What about this one?"

"Oh, the library?" She touched the screen, which enlarged the image. "Yes, we can run that one."

Jay smiled and straightened in the chair. "I'll take it."

Vivian manipulated the screen. "I can get the machine started from here." After about a minute, she turned back to Jay. "Now, about arranging the furniture...."

"I have some of my own, but not a lot."

"You can keep anything that's already in here, or have it moved out in favor of yours. We also have a storage room with more tables, cabinets, lamps, and such." She touched the screen again. "Let me show you."

By the time Madeline came back for him, Jay had made his furniture selections, as well.

Chapter 4

His coworkers insisted he sit while they packed and carried out his belongings. This they did very efficiently. Stephanie had put on her exoskeleton to carry the heaviest items.

"We've moved each other often enough," L. M. explained when Jay complimented them.

As Ginnie Mae and Terry reached for his 36-inch flat-screen television, Jay said, "Since you're giving me a new 60-inch TV, just take that to apartment 3A. Mary Price has a very old tube TV, and I want her to have it."

"Will do," Terry said, and picked up the flat-screen.

"Girlfriend?" Vivian asked from the kitchen.

"No, just a neighbor. And I want the bed to go to 4B. The Adamsons are just starting out and they're sleeping on an air mattress on the floor."

"Maybe they like it," L. M. said.

"No, I talked to them. It's because beds are so damned expensive. I didn't realize how expensive they were until I bought my first one."

"I'll say," Madeline said as she carried a box to the door.

She met Don coming in. "Hi, Madeline."

"Hi, Don. Excuse me." She walked out.

Don stepped in and walked over to Jay. "I came to see how you were doing."

"Still a bit washed out, but otherwise okay."

He looked around. "Moving in to the company mansion?"

"Yes. It seems someone broke in and switched my medication. I'm not opening myself up to that again."

"Any idea who?"

L. M. looked over at Don and shook her head.

Jay noticed L. M.'s motion but continued talking to Don. "Not specifically, no."

Don took a breath. "Need any help?"

L. M. lifted a box. "Thanks, we got this."

Don shrugged. "I'll get out of the way, then. See you at the bar, Jay?"

"Maybe. Maybe not. It'll be a while if I do."

Don patted Jay's upper arm. "Good luck, then, buddy."

When Jay's apartment was empty, he and Yolanda went to the landlord's office to give notice. Yolanda wrote a check covering Jay's rent to the end of his lease.

Ginnie Mae drove the moving truck back toward the company's residence; Irene rode with her. The rest of them piled in the company's SUV and followed. Madeline drove.

L. M. was in the front passenger seat. "Shall we wave at Charles's observer as we pass by?"

"No, let's just pretend we don't know he's there."

Jay leaned forward. "Charles's men are watching us?"

"Coming and going," L. M. said.

"Why pretend?" Jean asked. "They know we're on to them."

L. M. smiled. "You know the drill: we know they're watching us. They know we know they're watching us. We know they know we know they're watching us. And so forth."

"That's how the game is played," Madeline said grimly.

Sumita cleared him for work on Tuesday, though she and Madeline recommended an extended lunch break for his first week back. Jay was allowed to put the phone system on automatic for the second hour. Instead of going outside, he ate lunch in the cave, by himself, within view of Arachne. He found the device's hum and soft glow soothing. At the far end of the cave, he saw flashes of light and heard the buzzing of acetylene torches applied to metal as Terry, assisted by Ginnie Mae and Athena, welded pieces to be used to construct Terry's latest robot. Elsewhere, around a corner and out of sight, he could hear the women's chorus singing.

He faced away from Arachne as he ate his lunch, then pulled out his ereader. The ereader had its own lighted screen, but as he toggled from page to page, he began to notice the light flickering. At first, he thought that the ereader's battery was running low, but the indicator showed it still had a half charge. Then, turning, he saw light flashes from Arachne. As he listened to the women's voices singing, he realized that it was flashing in time to the music.

He placed the ereader on his chair and rushed to the room where the chorus was assembled.

"Are you all right, Jay?" Brittany asked, and the women stopped.

Jay pointed behind him. "It's Arachne. You have to see this."

Stephanie broke out into a run, sprinting past Jay. The others followed at a trot. When they caught up with her, they looked up at Arachne.

"Looks just the same to me," L. M. said.

"When you were singing, the light was flashing in tune to the melody."

"Okay, let's test this out." With a sweeping motion of her arm, she invited the others to assemble. "Was it doing it during our last song?" she asked Jay.

He nodded.

"Okay, we'll repeat." She waved her arms and they began singing "Turn the Beat Around" again.

For a moment, Jay was afraid Arachne would do nothing and he would appear foolish. But no, a few bars into the song, it began flashing and the humming changed pitch.

The women stopped singing.

"Well, I'll be doggone," Vivian said.

"Just a minute, just a minute," Stephanie said, and ran off. She came back carrying an electronic keyboard. Setting it in front of Arachne, she turned it on and played a chord. Nothing.

"B-flat, b-flat." L. M. stepped next to Stephanie and played several chords. Arachne responded: its light brightened around its edges and intensified in the middle, sometimes with red or blue tinges. The pitch of the hum also changed, going from higher to lower or lower to higher.

L. M. turned to Stephanie. "There's your multi-point code."

Stephanie smiled and rubbed her hands together. "I think we're on to something here."

"What do the colors mean?" Vivian asked.

"Well," Stephanie said, "if it's a Doppler shift, red means the light is going away from us and blue means it's coming toward us."

"Higher pitch toward us, lower pitch away from us," Nadia added.

The rest of the lunch break was taken up experimenting. Stephanie played chords, L. M. tried songs. Each of the women singers soloed to see if voices made a difference. They did: with some voices the light had blue tinges, other times red tinges; sometimes the light was intense, other times it was faint; sometimes the hum was high-pitched, other times the pitch was low.

"Let's try an untrained singer." L. M. turned to Jay. "Jay, you're up."

"Me? I can't sing."

"Try 'Take Me Out to the Ballgame.' I'm sure you sing that every seventh inning at the ballpark."

Since Jay could not deny that, he began to sing. Arachne sang back, as if humming along, and the light intensity and color changed as the tune did.

"Not bad," L. M. said. "Your voice is good enough for around-the-campfire singing."

Stephanie faced Arachne. "It seems to respond no matter who's singing."

Nadia stepped up to the keyboard. "I wonder if we can program a sequence that gives us a specific response."

L. M. checked her watch, then turned to Stephanie and Nadia. "You two go for it. The rest of us have to get back to our desks. Call if you need backup."

The next week, Madeline came up to Jay's desk in the afternoon. Athena and L. M. walked past her and out the door to a blue sporty car: an Airhawk.

"We're on alert, Jay," Madeline said as Athena drove away. "Keep an eye out for Athena and L. M. coming back. They may need assistance."

"Will do. Am I looking for anything in particular?"

Madeline turned from the parking lot to Jay. "We're shipping in a custom-made part from Symphony Robotics. Charles wants it too...or at least he wants to be sure we don't get it. We had them send the package to be picked up at the airport. We're hoping his observer thinks that Athena and L. M. are just out for a drive."

"The observer won't follow them?"

"So far, the observers have stayed in one place, and watch us go in and out." Madeline walked out the inner door and looked out the windows. Jay noted that the company SUV had been parked near the main entrance.

With Madeline's attention elsewhere, Jay did his best to see if he could track Athena and L. M. He had both their cell numbers, so tried that first. L. M.'s seemed elusive, but he managed to ping Athena's phone. He sat watching as they neared the municipal airport.

Madeline came back in and Jay quickly and quietly switched out the tracking screen to the monitor screen. She leaned over his desk. "Have they made it to the airport yet?"

Jay looked up, startled.

Madeline smiled.

Jay switched the screen back and indicated the display with a wave of his hand. "See for yourself."

She examined the screen and nodded. "Tell me when they're in view. I'll be in the car."

Jay watched as the dot on the screen went into the airport, and then started coming back. Just after they excited the freeway and got on the access road, they sped up.

He ran out to Madeline, who had the driver's window down. "Trouble."

"Get in."

Jay ran to the other side, scrambled in, and buckled up. She gunned the engine as soon as they were out of the parking lot. Through the windshield, he could see Athena speeding toward them, pursued by a black SUV. The blue car wove from side to side, but the SUV stuck with it, then passed it and cut it off. Athena turned the car to avoid a collision and slid off the road. The tires spun in the sand. Once the SUV stopped, seven men rushed out toward the blue car. Athena and L. M. remained where they were as the men beat on the car with crowbars, pulled on the doors, and rocked it back and forth, trying to gain entry. As Madeline drew even and stopped, he could see L. M. mocking the attackers with gestures.

"Grab a knife." Madeline indicated a box of large hunting knives. She took one and lunged from the car.

Jay, not trusting himself, or an opponent to wrench a knife from him and use it on him, scrambled out and ran to the nearest man on L. M.'s side of the blue car. He grabbed the attacker around the neck, to try to drag him away. Somehow the man escaped from his grip, turned, and faced him.

A shot echoed. The man's head exploded. Jay expected to be hit with blood and parts of brain, bone, and flesh, but instead, there seemed to be clay bits embedded with wires and pieces of circuit board stuck on his shirt, pants, arms, and neck. He looked back toward company headquarters to see Ginnie Mae kneeling on the roof of the entrance, aiming a high-powered rifle with a telescopic sight. She shot again, and again Jay was showered with mud. He looked across the roof of the car to see that Madeline's knife also had rust-colored clay on it. After Ginnie Mae shot a third time, Madeline faced the remaining figure, who turned and ran to his SUV, racing away with a squealing of wheels.

Jay knocked on L. M.'s window. "Are you all right?" he shouted.

L. M. rolled down the window. "We're fine. Ginnie Mae and Madeline got the simulacrums, and the human turned tail."

Jay heard a loud whirring sound and looked up.

"Drones," Madeline said. "Charles isn't finished yet."

Athena and L. M. got out of the car, watching the drones approach.

WHAM! A drone exploded in a ball of flame. Again, Jay looked toward the roof of company headquarters and saw Jean aiming the "weed killer" gun.

L. M. smiled and adjusted the toothpick in her mouth. "Yeah, it kills weeds real good." No sooner were the words spoken when a second drone exploded, then a third, a fourth, and a fifth. They were all gone.

Jay turned around, scanning the sky, but saw nothing else. "Is that it?"

"For now, I hope," Madeline said.

"We have the package," Athena said.

Madeline inhaled sharply. "Good. Let's get it inside and secured. Then we can come back for your car and clean up the simulacrum parts."

Jay watched as Athena reached inside the car and grabbed a plain brown box with an address label on it. She examined her car briefly as she walked to the company SUV. The Airhawk had surprisingly little damage for such a fierce assault. Even the windshield had remained intact.

Athena turned to him with a smile. "As I said, I put a lot of enhancements on my car."

Madeline pulled towels out of a box from the rear of the SUV and shut the hatchback. She tossed a towel to Jay. "Here. Remove all the mud you can and when we get back to the main building we can take the tunnel to the residence and clean up. We'll have Zoe scrub the SUV later."

Once inside the SUV, as Madeline drove to headquarters, Jay said, "I admire your ability to tell which ones are the simulacrums."

L. M. leaned forward. "We lived with them for about six months as Terry developed them, so we learned how to spot them. She even brought some to staff meetings. Lost a lot of receptionists that way—the simulacrums creeped them out and they quit."

He turned to Madeline. "How did you know I wouldn't take a knife and go after the human? I can't tell."

"I went after the human first and disarmed him right away," Madeline said.

"Good. I was afraid one of them would pull a gun and shoot us."

"They wouldn't do that," Madeline said. "If they killed someone, there'd be a police investigation, and Charles doesn't want the authorities looking into his business."

"What about the threats he made earlier, to us and our families?"

"Hot air," L. M. said. "He thinks we're a bunch of weak dames who can be frightened with threats."

"Those drones seemed pretty deadly."

Athena leaned toward him. "Oh, they probably could have shot around us, or laid down tear gas or dust to get us scattered and confused so the human or one of the simulacrums could get the package."

"Well, I'm glad we got it," Jay said.

Madeline smiled.

The day that they were to send Widget, the hamster, through Arachne, Jay arranged to be there to watch. Terry had put together a remote-controlled wagon to put the hamster cage on. She held Widget lovingly in her hands and stroked her fur.

"Now, don't be afraid, Widget. Everything will be fine."

Stephanie and Nadia stood next to Sumita. Stephanie had a smartphone in her hand. "Ready, Jean? We're about to send Widget through."

"I'm ready," Jean said.

"See?" Terry leaned over to look into Widget's face. "Jean is at the Yeager family estate, ready to fly you home."

Sumita sighed. "Okay, Terry, time to put Widget in and let her go through."

Terry placed Widget in the cage and closed the door. The hamster made for the food bowl and began to stuff her cheeks.

Nadia leaned over the laptop on the stand in front of her. Jay heard several tones and looked up and around.

"That's what Symphony Robotics gave us," Stephanie explained. "They specialize in music analysis hardware and software."

"Start the wagon, Terry," Sumita insisted.

Terry hit her remote. The wagon began to move. She walked alongside it all the way to the Arachne's entrance. "Don't be afraid, Widget. It's okay."

Widget showed no distress whatsoever, continuing to gobble up the hamster meal. Then, silently, the wagon with the hamster cage disappeared. Jay had expected Arachne to make more noise or for Arachne's lights to change color or intensity. But the light remained the same, and the tones Nadia fed it remained steady.

Stephanie's smartphone buzzed.

"She's through," Jean said.

Terry rushed over and spoke into Stephanie's phone. "Is she all right?"

"She's fine. Running on her hamster wheel. I'll get her home right away."

A little under an hour later, Jean's jet landed on the company's airstrip and taxied into its hangar stall in the cave complex. Jay was back at his desk, but now that he was a member of the company, he was able to activate the monitor in the hangar to see and hear what was going on.

Jean left the plane, hamster cage under her arm. She handed the cage to Sumita. "Widget hasn't stopped running since I picked up the cage at the Yeager estate."

"Does that mean something's wrong with her?" Terry asked.

"Not necessarily," Sumita said. "It may be that Arachne just gave her a burst of energy, like feeding her caffeine."

"Arachne is a high-energy device," Stephanie reminded her.

Jay then got distracted with a call and turned off the monitor. He did not get a chance to talk to Sumita again until she walked past his desk at the end of the day.

"How's Widget?" he asked.

"Oh, she's fine," Sumita said. "She settled down soon enough and took a nap. Easier for me to give her an MRI and CT scan and examine her. Stephanie and I think that going through Arachne just gave her a jolt of energy, that's all."

"What would it do to a human?" he asked.

She considered. "We're larger, so the same dose of energy may have a lesser effect on us. We may not feel it at all."

"So we're sending a human through next?"

Stephanie paused on her way out the door. "No, we're going to see if we can send things the other way through Arachne first."

"Then we might try some large mammals before going through ourselves," Sumita said.

"What sort of animal did you have in mind?" he asked.

"I can think of a couple of livestock species that would work," Sumita said. "When the time comes, we'll see if the Yeagers can buy one for their farm. It's mostly a dairy and horse ranch, along with some chickens."

On the day of the test, Jean flew Madeline, L. M., Stephanie, Terry, Nadia, Daphne, and Sumita to the Yeager estate. At the staff meeting where this plan was discussed, Jay wondered aloud about sending so many of the company's staff to one place, but Madeline and L. M. assured him that they had taken plenty of security precautions.

Athena, Ginnie Mae, and Jay stood next to Arachne. They each had a smartphone connected to someone on the Yeager estate. All were on speaker so they could hear each other.

"Okay, I'm going to throw a disk in," Stephanie announced.

Athena ushered Ginnie Mae and Jay to the side of Arachne. "Go ahead."

An object came through like a rocket and hit the far wall of the cave with a BANG that echoed in the chamber. Sparks flew.

"What did you do, shoot it out of a cannon?" Athena said.

"No, all I did was throw it like a discus."

"Well, your energy enhancer must have sped it up, then. Hold off while Ginnie Mae and I check for damage."

They walked away to the far end of the cave.

"At least it came through on our end," Jay said.

After a couple of minutes, he heard Athena speaking through the phone system. "Nothing in the cave was struck, but it hit a rock wall and smashed the disk. Try tossing it more gently this time. Ginnie Mae and I will move to the side and take the long way back."

After a moment, Stephanie called, "Ready?"

Jay squeezed against the side of Arachne's frame. "Go ahead."

This time the disk came through and hit the floor about ten feet in front of Arachne. Jay walked over and picked it up. "Okay, I got it."

"How does it look?" Stephanie asked.

He examined it closely. "Looks okay to me."

"Are the red indicators on?"

"Yes, there are a bunch of numbers here."

"Good. What are they?"

"Four...one...uff da." Jay heard a clatter on the stone floor behind him, and something nudged his right shoulder blade.

"Uff da...what?" Stephanie's voice said.

Jay turned, thinking that Stephanie had tossed in other disks. Instead, he found himself facing a black-and-white cow.

"Moo," it said.

Through his phone, Jay heard a male voice. "Lyr, is Clover there with you?"

L. M. called back, "No, Uncle Zach."

The cow had a tag on its ear with a printed number and a handwritten name under the number. Jay read it. "Clover's right here with me."

"What?" he heard several voices exclaim.

Clover nudged him again. "Moo."

"That's Clover, all right," the male voice said. "Are you experimenting with my cows?"

"No, Uncle Zach," L. M. said.

"Uh, what do I do?" Jay asked.

"See the harness on her head?" L. M. told him. "Grab it and lead her to Arachne. Then pat her near her rump and she should walk through."

"Okay." Jay took the harness and began to walk to Arachne. Clover's tail went up and he heard a "splat, splatter, splat" sound. He tilted his head back briefly as the stink reached his nose.

"Uh, Clover's taken a dump on the floor," he explained.

"Don't touch it; I want to analyze it!" Sumita shouted.

"Whatever you say." He found Clover to be compliant; he led her right to Arachne. He let go of the harness and patted her backside, being careful not to touch the area close to the tail. Clover plodded through and disappeared.

"There she is," the male voice said.

"Mr. Yeager," Daphne said, "do you have a separate container for each cow's milk or do you put it all together in one tank?"

"Yes, I separate them," he said. "Each cow's milk tastes different, and I want a particular taste for a particular ice cream."

"Have you pasteurized Clover's milk from this morning?"

"Not yet, no. I haven't had time."

"Let me have a cup or two to take with me. We'll send Jean back to you tomorrow to get tomorrow's milk."

"You think there might be something wrong with it?" he asked.

"Just checking," Daphne said. "I'm sure it will be fine, but don't use tomorrow's milk for ice cream until I have the results of the analysis."

"Well, I'm not happy with this," Zach said. "I was given to understand that you wouldn't be messing with my cows."

"You're right, Mr. Yeager," Madeline said. "This wasn't supposed to happen, and we didn't intend it to happen. I apologize."

"Clover is my best milker, and I breed her every year. She's one of my most valuable cows."

"In that case," Sumita said, "I wish to ask if I could take a DNA sample now and have the DNA sample the vet took the last time you bred her for comparison."

Jay heard a heavy sigh. "There better not be anything wrong, or I'm voting against your being here at the next family meeting."

"I apologize again, Mr. Yeager," Madeline said. "We'll do everything we can to make this right."

"We will, Uncle Zach," L. M. promised. "I'm sure everything will be just fine."

"We'll see," he said reluctantly.

Jay spoke into the smartphone. "Can I ask a silly question?"

"Ask any kind of question you want," Madeline said.

"How did a cow get through Arachne?"

"Um, I'm wondering about that, too," Stephanie said. "All I can come up with is that Arachne's destination portal must be a lot wider than we thought it was."

Jay heard Madeline's voice. "We're through here for today. Jay, tell Athena and Ginnie Mae that you're no longer on alert."

"Will do."

Athena and Ginnie Mae returned to find Jay cleaning his hands with wipes and circling the pile of manure. Ginnie Mae took one look and laughed.

"Sumita says to leave it for her," Jay explained.

Athena pinched her nose. "Now you know why I didn't go into the biological sciences."

Chapter 5

Jay again got wrapped up in phone calls and was not able to question his co-workers when they returned from the Yeager estate. He knew, however, that he would probably get answers at the next staff meeting.

Madeline seemed to want answers, too. She started the meeting by turning to L. M. "How's your Uncle Zach?"

"Oh, Aunt Thelma and Uncle Ned calmed him down after we left."

"Since the milk from before and after Clover walked through Arachne was chemically identical," Daphne said, "I called Mr. Yeager and told him to go ahead and use it."

"DNA was identical, too," Sumita said. "Nothing irregular about the manure, either."

"Uncle Zach told me to say he was sorry he overreacted, and that Clover's milk tastes even better now, so he's satisfied."

Daphne's brow furrowed. "But it's chemically identical. It should taste just the same."

L. M. shrugged.

"Any behavioral changes in Clover?" Brittany asked.

L. M. shook her head. "She's still a happy, contented cow."

"If she's even less stressed than before, that could affect the cortisol levels," Sumita suggested.

"But it's chemically identical," Daphne repeated softly.

Stephanie held out her hands as if balancing something in them. "Same chemicals, yes, but perhaps slight variations in amounts or proportions?"

"Could be, I suppose," Daphne said. "Within the margin of error."

"In any event," Madeline said, "our inadvertent large mammal experiment seems to have been a success. Any reason not to try to send one of us through next?"

The women looked from one to the other. "I don't see why not," Sumita said.

"Good." Madeline turned to Nadia and Stephanie. "Put together a plan and get it to me when you have it."

"After that," Jean said, "I want to determine the exact width of the destination portal."

"We haven't forgotten," Stephanie assured her.

Madeline nodded. "Yes, we don't want anything or anyone going through that we hadn't intended to go through."

"What I'm thinking," Jean said, "is that if it's wide enough, we can set three-dimensional destination coordinates in the air. I can fly the plane through it. It would certainly save us a lot of time getting halfway across the globe, if need be."

"And fly back through Arachne here?" Stephanie said. "The plane would enter the cave at astonishing speed. You'd end up as a stain on the cave wall."

"I'm willing to work on the issues of inertia," Jean said. "There must be some way to address them."

"Just for the record," Athena said, "I designed STACY to drive through Arachne."

Madeline looked from Jean to Athena. "First things first. Before we send any human-operated vehicles through, we have to determine whether a human can survive it."

In addition to handling the phones, one of Jay's responsibilities was to sort and deliver the mail. Since the local carrier put all the personal mail into boxes at the residence, and since most business was conducted through the Internet and the phones, the carrier had little to deliver at headquarters. Some days he did not stop at the company building at all. But this day, the carrier came in and handed Jay a large envelope addressed to Terry marked PRIVATE. After the carrier left, he took the envelope and started toward the entrance to the cave complex. On the way, he saw Irene, Yolanda, and Vivian coming back from choir practice.

He met Irene first. "Is Terry back there?"

"Yes. Watch out for the robot."

"Oh, is it done?"

She nodded and continued to her office.

He met Yolanda next. "Going to the secure area?" she
asked.

He nodded.

"Mind the robot."

"Okay, thanks."

Yolanda walked away; Vivian approached. "Be careful; Terry's
new robot is on the floor."

"So I've heard."

He pressed his thumb on the security pad and the door
opened. When he stepped through, the door closed behind
him. Normally, it took a few seconds for his eyes to adjust to
the cave's light level, but this day it seemed unusually dim.
The ramp had rows of tiny lights on each side, the same as
the ones in the aisles of passenger planes, so he knew where
to step safely. Nonetheless, when he reached the floor, he still
had trouble getting his bearings. He thought of reaching for the
smartphone in his pocket and turning on the flashlight, but
surely his eyes would make the adjustment in a few seconds?
He took a couple of tentative steps to one side and bumped into
something. Turning, his first impression was that this was a
wall. Maybe someone had installed partitions without telling
him? He reached out and touched the barrier. It seemed metallic.
The shape grew clearer; his eyes were adjusting—good. But it
seemed to be...a claw? Attached to...a foot? A very large foot.
Slowly, he leaned back and tilted his head to look toward the
ceiling.

"Ye gods!" he gasped.

"You okay, Jay?" Nadia's voice said.

He took a moment to remember to inhale and take some
deep breaths.

"Jay? Are you all right?" Stephanie called.

"Yeah...I just didn't expect...."

"Oh," Nadia said. "Someone should have warned you about
the robot."

He crouched, put his hands on his knees, and continued to
take deep breaths. "They did. I just didn't imagine..."

"...the monster who ate Pittsburgh?" Nadia prompted.

"Cincinnati," Stephanie said. "The monster who ate Pittsburgh
was a water monster. It came out of the river."

"Well, the monster who ate Cincinnati came out of the Ohio River."

Ginnie Mae walked up. "It was the same monster. They made the Pittsburgh movie first, and it was so popular they made the Cincinnati movie."

"Are you sure?" Stephanie asked.

Ginnie Mae nodded. "I saw each of them twice."

"Oh, yeah," Nadia said. "I remember now."

Terry walked up. She was wearing a garment reminding him of the motion-capture outfits that actors wore: black with shiny metallic discs at her joints.

"Say, Terry," Stephanie said, "did you model your robot after the monster who ate Cincinnati?"

"Or Pittsburgh?" Nadia added.

Before Terry could answer, the door at the top of the ramp opened and closed, illuminating the cave area for a few seconds. Jay glanced up again and saw he had not overreacted—the robot was indeed that horrifying.

Madeline's voice said, "Terry, the robot is blocking the light. Either move it or turn up the illumination."

Terry took out a remote and the lights went up.

Jay stole another glance at the robot and winced.

"I'm really sorry, Jay. I didn't mean for it to scare you. I'll move it back," Terry offered.

Jay waved his hands. "Give me a moment, please," he squeaked.

"Okay," Terry said. "Sorry again."

"Don't worry about it; I'll live," he reassured her.

Ginnie Mae chuckled and put her hands on her hips. "Jay, it's just a robot."

"It still gives me the creeps," he said.

By this time Madeline had reached floor level. "It's supposed to."

Jay realized that he still held an envelope for Terry. To delay her, he extended it to her. "I almost forgot. This is for you."

She smiled and took it. "Oh, good. This is the sound chip that will make the robot roar."

Somewhere, Madeline had found a chair and set it next to Jay. "Here, Jay, have a seat."

He sank into it gratefully. "Thank you."

Terry turned to Nadia and Stephanie. "I modeled it after the Atomic Test Horror."

Jay raised a hand. "I saw that movie." He waved toward the robot. "This is scarier."

"Of course, I couldn't duplicate it exactly," Terry explained. "Copyright issues."

"Still, it looks as if it could devour Pittsburgh," Nadia said, and walked away.

"Or Cincinnati," Stephanie said, and followed.

"What are you going to name it?" Ginnie Mae asked.

Terry looked up at it. "Nightmare."

Ginnie Mae nodded. "That's good enough."

Terry turned around, holding the envelope high. "I guess I'll put this away and come back and move the robot."

Ginnie Mae extended a hand. "Here, I'll put it on your desk."

Terry gave her the envelope. "Thanks."

After Ginnie Mae left, Madeline asked, "Was that sound chip from Symphony Robotics?"

"Yes. Why?"

"How did you get it past Charles's spies?"

Terry smiled. "I remembered that the engineering department at my alma mater uses them all the time. So I asked a former professor if he would order an extra and send it to me if I reimbursed him. He said he was about to mail out the alumni newsletter and would put it in there. The envelope had the university's return address."

Madeline patted Terry on the back. "Good thinking."

"Thank you." Terry turned to Jay. "Okay with you if I move it now?"

He waved at her. "Go ahead."

She touched a metal bracelet on her wrist. When she moved her arm, the robot moved its arm in the same way. The robot's joints cracked as it moved, making a sound as if it were breaking tree trunks. She walked; the robot walked. The robot's feet pounded the floor; Jay felt the vibrations through the chair legs. The huge eyes glowed orange. The wide mouth opened and closed when Terry's did, displaying long ragged teeth resembling knife shards. The robot's arms were not short T. Rex arms, but long, thick, supple arms ending in paws bristling with ridges and claws. Spikes protruded from nearly every square foot of its metallic robot hide down to the ankles. Its outside had been painted a sickening shade of green. As it moved, he noted that the neck could extend or contract to a degree, and that it could crouch or move with its head high. Crouched, it could easily pass through Arachne's gate; walking with head high, it could reach the top of the cave complex. The legs were long enough for it to straddle a two-lane highway, at the least.

Jay turned to Madeline, who appeared to be admiring Terry's handiwork. "May I ask what you're going to use that for?"

"To scare the pants off of our enemies, of course."

Jay nodded. "That'll work."

Everyone wanted to be in the vicinity when L. M. went through Arachne, but someone needed to mind the store, and Madeline told Jay he was to stay at watch at his desk. Besides, he could see everything that was going on through one of his monitors. As for the others, they were told to stay at their posts until just before L. M. went through. Sumita had gathered "before" data to compare with "after" data. She had spent some time taking L. M.'s vitals, drawing blood, measuring lung capacity, and so forth, before flying with Jean to the Yeager estate.

L. M. had been selected because of her perfect pitch. Though Nadia put the tonal chords L. M. would need into the smartphone she would carry, Stephanie and L. M. also wanted her to sing the notes, and were not satisfied until the computer said that the sounds matched perfectly. Arachne hummed in tune during the rehearsal and brightened with the rhythm. Last of all, Stephanie and Nadia put a band around L. M.'s head with a camera that would record everything L. M. saw and heard.

When L. M. was ready, Madeline came onto the main floor, waving Irene, Yolanda, and Vivian through the security door ahead of her.

Jay made sure that his primary monitor showed everything around Arachne, and that a secondary monitor was tied into L. M.'s camera's signal.

L. M. stood in front of Arachne, looking it over.

"Lose the toothpick, L. M.," Madeline said.

She sighed and put it into her pocket.

"Jean and I are waiting at the destination portal," Sumita said to her though Madeline's smartphone. "If you feel sick or weak after going through, we'll fly you back."

"Got it," L. M. said.

"If you get stuck," Stephanie said, "sing."

"What if I can't?" L. M. teased.

"Then use the phone," Madeline said. "Good luck."

L. M. rolled her shoulders, stretched out her arms, jumped up and down a couple of times, and took a deep breath. "Well, if Clover could do it, so can I. Here goes nothing." She held out her own smartphone and pressed the tone app. Arachne came to life with a bright white light and a strong hum. L. M. stepped toward it with purposeful strides and disappeared.

Immediately, Nadia and Stephanie gathered around the laptop. "No camera signal," Stephanie said.

Jay was puzzled, too. The camera on L. M.'s forehead had shown Arachne ahead of her right up until the moment L. M. stepped in. Then it went blank. All Jay could see was a white screen, and he guessed that was all the others were seeing, too.

Madeline picked up her smartphone. "Jean, Sumita, L. M. just stepped through. What are you seeing?"

"Nothing yet," Jean said through Madeline's phone.

"She should go right through," Stephanie said. "Clover did."

Madeline turned to Stephanie. "Can you call her?"

"Through her smartphone? Sure." Stephanie dialed a number on the laptop. She shook her head. "Signal not getting through. No connection. No ring tone on the other end."

Madeline lifted her phone again. "Jean?"

"Nothing, Madeline."

"Do we go after her?" Vivian asked.

"Not until we know what's going on." Madeline turned to Stephanie and Nadia. "Is there any kind of tracking you can do?"

"Nothing. No signal. I've tried," Nadia said.

"Wait a minute," Jean's voice said. "There she is!"

Sure enough, the monitor tracking the camera on L. M.'s head focused on Jean in her flight suit and Sumita wearing her lab coat, standing on the landing strip on the Yeager estate in front of the plane.

They all cheered, applauded, and hugged each other. Jay stood, held up his arms, and cheered. Then he realized he was alone and sat down again with a wide grin.

"Damn!" L. M.'s voice came through Jean's phone. "That was an experience!"

Jean reached up, grabbed the camera off L. M.'s head, and aimed it at her so they could see her.

"Are we glad to see you," Madeline said. "What was the holdup?"

"When I got in there, everything was white. There was nothing to take my bearings. No landmarks, nothing. I stopped and looked around. I thought I'd see Jean and Sumita ahead of me or you behind me, but nothing. Finally I thought I'd just keep going forward in the direction my toes were pointing, and suddenly, I saw Jean and Sumita and I was here."

"Did you get a call on your smartphone?" Stephanie asked.

L. M. took hers and checked it. "No notice of any calls at all."

"How do you feel?" Sumita asked.

L. M. smiled. "Energized! As if I could run a marathon and not get tired."

Sumita stepped forward and took L. M. by the arm. "Okay, let's get into the plane and I'll check you out."

About a half hour later, L. M. and Sumita descended from the plane. L. M. was rolling her shirt sleeve back over her forearm.

Sumita talked into her cellphone. "She's fine, Madeline. I'll have to wait until I get to the lab to analyze the entire run of tests, but I don't see why she can't come back."

L. M. leaned over and talked into Sumita's phone. "Ready and raring to go. Someone is going to have to make a return trip at some point. Might as well be now."

"Okay," Madeline said. "Use that energy and come on back. Don't pause this time; just walk on through."

"Whatever you say." L. M. held out her hand; Jean gave her the band with the camera. Jay saw the view swing around to an attractive part desert, part prairie vista—he admired the Yeager family's taste in scenery. Then the monitor showed nothing but white again. He turned his attention to the primary monitor, where Madeline and the others waited for L. M.'s return. Within seconds, L. M. stumbled out of Arachne. Madeline and Ginnie Mae surged forward and caught her before she fell.

L. M. straightened up, breathing heavily. "Thanks!"

"What happened this time?" Stephanie asked.

"I'm concerned about your breathing," Brittany said. "Did you do anything different?"

By now, L. M. had stopped huffing and puffing. "Something pushed me. It was like a hurricane-force wind at my back, but there was no wind."

"Was it like a hand pushing your back?" Nadia asked.

"No, the pressure was even from my heels to the top of my head. It was like Arachne giving me a mighty shove out the door."

Meanwhile, Jay ran a replay on this secondary monitor. The live feed had shown the scenic vista, then white, then Madeline standing in front of L. M. Now it showed a scenic vista, then L. M.'s shoes against a field of white – she was apparently looking down briefly—then Madeline standing in front of L. M.

"I've got something," Stephanie announced.

The others gathered around her laptop. She played it again.

L. M. pointed to the screen. "Yes, that's what happened."

"Why didn't the live feed show L. M.'s view inside Arachne?" Ginnie Mae asked.

"Just as we couldn't get the smartphone signal through to L. M. when she was within Arachne," Stephanie said, "I think the camera can't transmit within Arachne. But it will record."

"Why didn't Arachne push her out from here to the Yeager estate?" Madeline asked.

"I can't explain that," Stephanie said. "Arachne must work differently going from origin to destination than it does the other way."

Madeline's phone rang.

"Shall we fly back now?" Jean asked.

"Yes, Jean, you and Sumita can come on back." Madeline turned to the others. "It seems we need to learn a lot more about Arachne. To start with, what causes the energy and optical phenomena? How wide—and tall—is the destination portal?"

"I'll get right on it," Stephanie said, "but it means we need to send more people through eventually."

Brittany leaned over to talk into Madeline's smartphone. "Sumita, I'll do the return physical here."

"Yes, that will save us some time," Sumita said. "See you soon."

Brittany took L. M.'s arm. "Let's go."

Jay ran into Sumita as he was taking out a pasta bowl in the company kitchen at the start of his lunch break. "If it doesn't go against medical confidentiality, how is L. M.?"

"In her own words, she's her same ornery self." Sumita smiled and poured a mug of coffee.

"Nothing different?"

She shook her head. "Nothing that current medical science can determine. Everything was the same: before she went through, when she arrived at the estate, and when she got back here...except for a rise in endorphins, but that's well within the usual limits."

"Then we can send more people through."

"Yes. It seems safe enough." She took a sip from the mug. "Weird, but safe."

Jay again sat at his post, watching through his monitors, at the next test. Nadia bent over a table that had two laptops on it and spoke to Madeline. "Okay. I've cloned Stephanie's laptop. Everything on her laptop is now on this one." She put a hand on one of the laptops. "If Stephanie loses her laptop, or doesn't come back, we'll still have all of her information."

Athena stood by, observing, with her arms crossed in front of her. "You'd better come back, or I'll have to take over the physics duties, at least until we can hire someone else, and I'm busy enough with the engineering projects."

Stephanie smiled and took the laptop that Nadia had just had her hand on. "Don't worry, I'll come back...but don't expect me to just walk in and walk out, either. I'm going to take my time."

Madeline checked her watch. "You have until dinnertime."

"How do we know that clocks don't stop within Arachne?" Athena asked.

"Because the engines worked," Stephanie said. "The vehicles we used to send the grasshoppers and frogs and Widget into Arachne were motorized, and they chugged right on through."

"I'll make sure she gets back," L. M. said.

Stephanie turned to Madeline. "Much as I enjoy L. M.'s company, I can do this by myself, Madeline."

"And if you get absorbed in the excitement of discovery and don't realize that eight hours have flown by?" She raised an eyebrow.

Stephanie sighed and hugged the laptop. "Okay, I see the point."

"Do you activate Arachne or do I?" L. M. asked Stephanie.

Madeline turned back to Nadia. "You know the sequence for the Yeager estate."

She nodded and sent out the tones.

"Remember, Jean is standing by at the Yeager estate in case your return is blocked," Madeline said.

L. M. turned back briefly as she and Stephanie walked toward Arachne. "Got it."

After they disappeared, Madeline said, "Nadia can keep watch here and let us know when they come back. Or Jay can let us know, from watching his monitor. The rest of us can get back to work."

Not five minutes later, Jay was startled by a sudden burst of light and sound coming through his monitor—as if someone had switched on a radio station playing John Philip Sousa. Facing the monitor, he saw Arachne producing a sound and light show: upbeat, bouncy music. It reminded him of houses lit up for the holidays when the sound and lights were synched. Nadia watched carefully, too—she looked alternately from Arachne to her laptop. He hoped she was getting good data to analyze.

He heard someone come up from behind him, and turned to see Irene, Yolanda, and Vivian huddled together, also focused on the monitor.

"Sounds as if they're having a party in there," Vivian said.

Madeline stepped through the staircase entrance and onto the floor. They all turned to her. She waved at them. "Come on, we can see it up close. I'll even relieve Jay for a while so he can take a look."

"But Arachne is so big," Irene said. "We can see it all at once on the TV."

"I'm good," Yolanda said.

"Besides, we're closer to the kitchen here," Vivian said.

Madeline smiled. "All right. But I want to see it live." She walked away.

The three remaining women rushed to their respective offices and wheeled their chairs toward Jay's station.

Jay tapped his pen on the side of the monitor. "That tune seems familiar, somehow, but I can't place it."

"I know what you mean," Yolanda said, "but I'm drawing a blank, too."

He turned around to Irene and Vivian, who shook their heads.

Jay hit the intercom. "Nadia?"

"Yes, Jay?"

"Does that tune ring a bell?"

"I'm trying to place it. I've put it through Symphony's song identification system, but nothing yet."

Madeline's voice said, "It could be its own unique tune. Songwriters come up with new music all the time."

"Well, if it finds something," Nadia said. "I'll let you know."

"Thanks." Jay closed the intercom.

Jay, Irene, Yolanda, and Vivian spent most of the rest of the afternoon watching the monitor. Madeline passed them on the way back to her office after about an hour, but everyone else remained in place. Occasionally, Jay needed to take a call, or Vivian went to get coffee for everyone, or someone needed to take a break, but otherwise they were there, observing and commenting.

"Wait. Was that a beep?" Jay remarked at one point.

"Crescendo. Decrescendo," Yolanda said at another.

Jean also called in around mid-afternoon. "Nadia, are you there?"

"I'm here," Nadia said.

"Stephanie and L. M. are testing out the width of the exit portal. They think they can adjust it."

"Good, that's what we want. Are you getting a light and sound show on your end?"

"No, Stephanie or L. M. just appear out of nowhere and disappear again."

"I'm recording it here," Nadia said. "You can see it when you get back."

"I'll take you up on it," Jean said.

About a half hour before official quitting time, the lights and sounds faded away, as if they had been played by a battery-powered radio that had used up its charge. Seconds later, L. M. stepped out of Arachne, dragging Stephanie by the arm. Stephanie carried her open laptop.

"You could have let me try it just one more time," Stephanie protested.

"Yeah, and there would have been one more thing after that, and one more thing after that. You gotta eat and sleep, you know, and so do I. Arachne will still be there tomorrow."

Nadia stood from where she sat behind the stand holding Stephanie's original laptop. "You didn't shoot out like a rocket this time."

L. M. put a hand in her pocket, took out a wrapped toothpick, unwrapped it, and put it in her mouth. "We figured it out."

Chapter 6

When L.M. let go of her, Stephanie scurried to the stand where Nadia bent over her laptop and set down the duplicate. "So much data to process!"

L. M. waved at the monitor camera. "Madeline, Jean is on her way back."

Jay saw Madeline emerge from the stairwell. She walked over, bent over his desk, and spoke into the intercom. "Thanks."

"You should have seen the light show here," Nadia said to Stephanie.

Stephanie turned to her and smiled. "You should have seen ours!"

Brittany walked up to the stand and put a hand on Stephanie's shoulder. "Let me make you supper, my place."

Stephanie kept her eyes on her laptop. "Just a sec. Need to write my notes before I forget."

Brittany smiled. "You won't forget."

Stephanie continued working on her laptop.

"I'll make Classified Pizza," Brittany offered.

At Jay's station, behind him, Irene clasped her hands and grinned. "Classified Pizza!"

Stephanie paused and looked up.

"But you have to go now," Brittany coaxed.

Madeline said through the intercom, "Is that an open invitation?"

Brittany turned to the monitor. "Sure."

"Okay, let's all knock off early and meet at Brittany and Sumita's place."

The apartments in the residence were roomy; still, Jay marveled that they all fit in the living room so easily. He picked up a photo on an end table showing Sumita and Brittany wearing wedding dresses, holding identical bouquets, and smiling at each other in front of an altar.

"Picture book wedding," Sumita said as Jay put the photo down. "Brittany made and decorated the cake herself."

Vivian leaned over. "I designed the dresses."

Jay nodded. "All beautiful."

"Dinner's ready!" Brittany called.

He got in line and took a plate. Two large pizzas, baked on cookie sheets, dominated the middle of the table. He used a wide spatula to pick up an ample slice, took the serving fork to add salad to his plate, passed up the beer, and took a root beer mug. Making his way to the living room, he sat in an empty wooden chair that reminded him of a professor's chair at the university. Others sat on the couches or on the floor on cushions. Irene took the lone bean bag chair.

For a time, they all munched with sounds of appreciation for the food.

"Ummmmmm." Jay turned to Brittany. "Heavenly. This is the best pizza I ever tasted. The crust is out of this world!"

Brittany smiled. "My secret recipe. That's why it's 'classified.'"

"The homemade salad dressing is to die for, too," Zoe said. She had paused on her way to her evening maintenance work to join the party.

"Hate to eat and run," Stephanie said, "but I need to go back and finish my notes."

"No you're not." L. M. grinned. "I locked all the doors from the inside." She nodded at Zoe. "Gave the master key card to Zoe. No one else is going back to work until morning...unless you want to trip the fire alarm, which would open all the doors and windows, but piss off everyone."

"You have a laptop in your room, don't you?" Nadia said.

"Plus an old-fashioned pad of paper and pencils?" L. M. prompted.

Stephanie sighed and settled back into her seat.

"Sleep will help you reinforce your memories," Madeline assured her.

"So will talking about it," Athena said. "Now tell us all what happened in there while Arachne was glowing."

Stephanie set her plate on a nearby table. "When L. M. and I got in there, it was just as she said: all white, no landmarks."

L. M. pinched the toothpick in her mouth. "Did you think I was making it up?"

Stephanie shook her head. "No, I was relating it as confirming evidence."

L. M. nodded. "Okay. Go on."

Stephanie turned to the others. "I opened up the laptop, and played a set of notes."

"A song," L. M. interjected.

Stephanie smiled. "Yes, and then it lit up! We could see everything! Jean on the Yeager estate, you guys in the cave."

"And other stuff, too," L. M. said.

"A third scene," Stephanie said. "I did a reverse, translating the harmony into GPS coordinates, and got a region outside Reno, Nevada."

Jean's face lit up. "A three-way corridor! Do you know what this means?"

"Yes," Madeline said. "It means we solved the problem of how to relocate people outside the company when we rescue them. Taking them back here would not be a secure option."

"It also means we can do point-to-point flight," Jean said. "I could take off here, enter Arachne, and emerge over Portland, for instance."

"...and have Portland air traffic control label you as a possible terrorist and scramble jets to shoot you down," Madeline said.

Jean tilted her head toward Athena. "Athena designed the plane to be stealthy. If I turn off the transponder, they won't know I'm there."

"There's still visual surveillance to account for, even if you turn on the concealing shield," Athena said. "They won't be able to read your tail number, but they'll think you're a UFO and possibly hostile."

Jean's smile never diminished. "I'm sure there's a way around that."

Ginnie Mae leaned toward Stephanie. "Go on with your story!"

"I gave L. M. the laptop, took my cell phone out of my pocket, and walked out the third portal."

Madeline inhaled sharply. "Without consulting us? Without one of our group being there to meet you in case something went wrong?"

Stephanie's face fell.

L. M. wriggled the toothpick. "Madeline, it's one thing to say that here when we're all settled, but you haven't been in there. Yeah, what you say makes sense, but when you're in there, you feel powerful, as if you can do anything and get away with it."

Brittany lifted an eyebrow. "That's something we're going to have to take account of in the future."

"Okay, L. M.," Madeline said. "You two took a chance and you got away with it...this time. I'll call 'no harm, no foul' for now." She nodded to Stephanie. "Stephanie, you still have the floor."

A wry smile appeared on Stephanie's face. "Well, I appeared exactly where the GPS on the laptop said I would. I confirmed it with my cell phone."

"Anyone see you?" Athena asked.

Stephanie shook her head. "Not a soul there."

"Then what?" Irene prompted.

"We tried other destinations." Stephanie glanced over to Athena. "I picked remote locations. Sometimes I went out, sometimes L. M. did."

"Then we started to see if we could map out the dimensions of the portal," Yeager said.

Stephanie grinned. "And we did! We found by 'fine-tuning' the melodies, we could make the portals larger or smaller."

"We went to where Jean was, and then back in, and then to a third location, and back to Jean," L. M. said.

"Why did L. M. just see white the first time?" Ginnie Mae asked.

Stephanie turned to Yeager and smiled. "That's because we had a two-way portal. Arachne seems to want a three-way portal, and when the third is closed off, there's a lack of transparency."

"Arachne's a machine, not an entity," Daphne said, looking bemused. "It can't 'want' anything."

"When a machine does things that remind people of human behavior, humans tend to apply human analogues to it," Brittany said. "Not sure there's any way around that."

Daphne threw her hands up in surrender.

"What about the lack of hurricane wind at your back when you came out?" Nadia asked.

"With a two-way portal," Stephanie explained, "Arachne acts like a funnel, with the cave entrance the narrow end and the destination portal the wide end. Going back, the force lines concentrate and push out."

"We can fix that with the three-point portal," L. M. said, "or even out the entrance and exit portal sizes."

"We can change the width of the in-between space, too," Stephanie said. "We can make it narrow or wide."

"What took you so long in there?" Vivian asked.

Stephanie grinned. "So many variables...the width of each portal, the location of the destination portals, the size of the in-between space...we were learning as we went along."

"At least the clocks were accurate within Arachne," L. M. said.

"I did lose track of time," Stephanie said, "but L. M. always reminded me how many hours had passed."

"Got that right."

Madeline put her plate on a low table and sat back on the couch. "Okay. Stephanie, you and L. M. are going to teach me, Nadia, Athena, Daphne, and Terry how to do this."

Stephanie blinked. "I don't know everything about it myself, yet."

L. M. turned to her. "Neither do I. We'll learn."

"And the rest of us will learn with you," Madeline said.

Brittany raised a hand. "I want in."

Madeline turned to her. "All right." She looked around. "Anyone else?"

No one else responded. Jay mused that he really had no desire to go into Arachne, interesting as it was. Besides, when Sumita said that it increased endorphin levels, that meant that it affected the brain, and while endorphins had a positive effect on most people, with his altered brain chemistry, it might not have the same effect. He did not wish to risk it.

Madeline turned to her right. "Nadia, give Jay the codes to our satellite surveillance cameras and show him how to use them."

She nodded.

Jay beamed. Now this was something he could sink his teeth into!

Madeline turned to him. "You're not to use them to watch baseball away games live."

He chuckled. "Don't worry, I won't."

"Not even the World Series?" Ginnie Mae asked.

Madeline sighed. "Well, check with me first."

Meanwhile, Sumita and Brittany had left the room. They returned: Sumita carrying a pitcher of beer, and Brittany carrying a large bottle of root beer.

"Anyone need their glasses topped off?" Sumita asked.

When the glasses had been refilled, Brittany lifted hers, and the others followed suit. "To Arachne!"

"Arachne!" the others echoed, and drank.

Jay became happily busy in the following days. Nadia sat next to him at his desk for an hour or two each day until he operated the satellite system as well as she could. The others immersed themselves in their own tasks.

One day, a stranger, a woman, walked into the front door. Puzzled, Jay checked his monitors. He had not seen a car drive up, and the monitors seemed to confirm it. When the woman walked through the inner door, and moved as if to continue past his desk, he quickly stood and positioned himself in front of her.

He smiled and held out his hand. "Jay Ecklund, receptionist. I'd be happy to sign you in and escort you to wherever you need to go."

She smiled. "I'm Daphne," said Daphne's voice.

He put his hand down and licked his lips. "May I see your company ID, please?"

She reached into a pants pocket. "Okay, but it won't match my face."

"That's okay. If you're Daphne, you'll have Daphne's ID..." He took the offered card and glanced at it. "...which you do." He handed it back and nodded. "Daphne, you're a real artist."

"Thank you."

* * *

The regular staff meeting was later that morning. Madeline was the last one in. As she sat at the table, she said, "L. M., lose the toothpick; Daphne, take off the mask."

Daphne peeled off the mask but held it in her hands.

Madeline turned to Yolanda. "You're up first, Yolanda."

Yolanda opened a folder in front of her. "The mini-robots are selling very well. The factory is working two shifts to keep up with demand, and the trade journals are calling it 'the toy of the year.' Every kid seems to want one...or a dozen."

Ginnie Mae held up a thumb. "Good."

Madeline nodded. "You and Terry did a great job designing those. Congratulations."

Yolanda turned to Vivian. "Sales of Vivian's new 'Your Happy Penguin' stuffed toy is approaching the phenomenal sales of 'Your Happy Teddy Bear.'"

Madeline turned to Vivian. "Nice work, Vivian."

Vivian beamed.

"The stuffed toys and the mini-robots," Yolanda continued, "along with all our other electronic and software products, are keeping our revenues at record levels."

Everyone applauded.

Madeline turned to Daphne, then Jay. "Daphne, you're next... and by the way Jay, nice catch."

Jay gave her a brief salute.

Daphne fingered the mask in front of her. "I had Nadia scan my face mask using the latest facial recognition software, and it did not match my own face in the database."

"Love it," L. M. said.

Daphne inclined her head to Jay. "As Jay can tell you, it looks perfectly natural and will blend in with your own skin tones. Easy to get on and off. Lets your skin breathe, too."

"Good work, Daphne." Madeline turned to Vivian. "Okay, Vivian."

She had a stack of papers and passed them around. "Those are the latest designs. Note that they're two-piece."

Jean held up the paper. "I still want a jumpsuit."

"I'll make you a jumpsuit," Vivian assured her. "And put in a fly on Jay's pair of pants. I think the rest of us would rather have something easy to take on and off when answering a call of nature."

Jay examined the drawings closely. The design seemed simple to him, though he was no fashion expert. The outfit appeared to consist of a simple long-sleeved, v-neck shirt with a collar, plus long pants. He noticed cuffs at the wrists and ankles. "Are these uniforms?"

Madeline nodded. "To be worn only when we're using Arachne for a rescue. To maintain our anonymity."

Jay leaned over in Madeline's direction. "Do you expect us all to go through?"

"You don't have to if you don't want to, Jay," Madeline assured him. "But we need to be prepared for any eventuality."

Jay nodded.

Madeline turned back to Vivian. "What about the fabric?"

She distributed fabric squares. "Athena needed to make some enhancements to my sewing machine and cutting equipment. Bullet-resistant fabric is a bear to work with."

Jay picked up his sample. It had a sheen to it, and appeared to change color when he held it up to the light.

"I couldn't make a coating to cause us to be invisible," Daphne said. "But any light shining on us will cause a reflective glare."

"What about at night?" L. M. asked.

"The fabric for the overcoat is treated to absorb light," Daphne said.

"Overcoat?" Jay asked.

Irene, sitting next to him, reached over and turned Jay's paper over. Jay whispered, "thanks."

"It's reversible for daytime use," Vivian said.

Madeline took one last look at the paper. "Good progress, everyone."

"Then I can start measuring people?" Vivian asked.

Madeline nodded, then turned to Athena. "Helmets?"

"Prototype's in the shop. I'll start measuring people, too."

"Footwear?" Jay asked.

Madeline indicated Daphne, Vivian, and Athena. "Working on it."

"I'm making gloves, too," Vivian added.

"Goggles eventually," Stephanie added. "Working on the optics now. Enhanced night and day vision."

Madeline turned to Athena. "Is the shield up yet?"

Athena leaned forward slightly. "Yes. There's one-way transparency that allows us to look into Arachne but won't allow anyone to see in to us. It doubles as a blast shield."

"Shield?" Jay asked.

"Stephanie said she could see the cave complex from within Arachne," Madeline said. "We don't want outsiders looking in, so I had Athena and Ginnie Mae put up a screen in front of Arachne's entrance."

"Also," Athena added, "if something comes through Arachne too quickly, it won't smash against the far side of the cave."

"Easy for us to walk around when we go in and out," Stephanie explained. "And even enough room for STACY to drive by and inside."

Madeline looked around the room. "Good work, everyone. We're making progress."

That afternoon, Madeline stopped at Jay's desk. "We're training Nadia on Arachne today. That means you'll have to work the satellites."

Jay looked up and smiled. "What do I do?"

Madeline leaned over and typed on Jay's keyboard. "This is the series of GPS coordinates we're going to emerge at, in order. Aim the satellite at each in turn. We'll call in and ask if you can see us, and then go back to Arachne and emerge at the next destination. You can do all that from here."

Jay slid the keyboard back within reach. "Will do."

"See you later," Madeline said, and left.

As usual when Arachne was in operation, Jay had a monitor trained on it. He had already turned a satellite to the first coordinate, a desolate location in Argentina, when Nadia and Madeline entered the portal. Not long after that, they emerged at the location. Nadia held her satellite phone and waved upward. "See me?"

"Yes, you and Madeline are in the picture," Jay said.

The two women disappeared. Jay turned his attention to the monitor of a second satellite, aimed at a location in the Sahara Desert. Soon, Madeline and Nadia walked out of the portal, and repeated the visual and sound check. Jay had just finished turning that satellite to the Gobi Desert when Nadia and Madeline reappeared. When they re-entered Arachne, Jay focused the satellite at a site in Western Australia. Again, the two women came out, checked in, and retreated.

That was the end of the list. Nothing happened for a while, though Arachne continued to issue lights and sound. Then he got an audio signal. "Jay?"

"Yes, Nadia?"

"We made an impromptu detour to Hawaii. Can you find us?"

"Give me a minute or so." He pinged her phone, got the GPS coordinates, and turned the satellite there. "Now I see you."

"Good work, Jay," Madeline said over the phone. "Tell Stephanie we're coming back home soon."

"Will do." He called Stephanie and then kept an eye on the cave complex monitor until Madeline and Nadia returned.

When Jay entered the conference room for the next staff meeting, he saw Jean already seated. She was dressed, as usual, in her flight suit. A folder lay open in front of her. He could not see at the distance and angle what it was, but she had a satisfied smile on her face as if she were a member of the debate team about to make an irresistible argument.

As usual, Madeline was the last to be seated. "L. M., lose the toothpick. Jean, yes, you can try to fly the plane through Arachne. Make a plan with Stephanie and put it on my desk."

Jean's mouth opened, then closed with a smile.

The day of the test, Madeline evacuated the cave complex except for Stephanie, who stood guard with her laptop at a right angle to Arachne's entrance. As a result of the evacuation, everyone else clustered around Jay's desk, watching the monitors. One focused on the outside, overlooking the company's landing strip. The company plane rested there; Jay could see Jean through the windshield. Another monitor showed the cave complex, with Stephanie standing ready. A third displayed a desolate snowy vista in Antarctica.

Madeline leaned over Jay to check the monitors. "Okay, Jean, take off. Stephanie, can you have the aperture open above the landing strip by the time Jean circles around?"

The plane reached the end of the strip and soared upward.

"It's on...now," Stephanie said.

"I'm ready for it," Jean's voice said through a speaker.

"Remember," Madeline said, "if you accidentally appear in the cave complex, eject immediately."

"Not gonna happen," L. M. mumbled behind them.

Madeline glanced in L. M.'s direction, then turned back to the monitors.

Even though he had overheard Stephanie and Jean conferring earlier about the exact height and dimensions of the projected portal aperture over the landing strip, and even though the drone test flights through it to the Yeager estate and back had been successful, Jay still felt nervous as Jean circled the airstrip. There was no sound in the room except the ceiling exhaust fan pumping in fresh air as Jean straightened out the plane. She flew straight above the landing strip...and disappeared.

Immediately, everyone's attention focused on the Antarctica monitor.

"Yes!" Jean exclaimed triumphantly as the plane appeared over the snowdrifts.

Jay let out a breath he had not realized he was holding. The others cheered and applauded.

"Any problems?" Madeline called into the speaker.

"None whatsoever," Jean said. "Coming home."

Madeline turned to the intercom. "Heads up, Stephanie."

"Aw, c'mon, Madeline, you don't really think that plane is going to rush into the cave, do you?"

Madeline turned to her. "The chances may be small, but they're not zero."

"Madeline," L. M. insisted. "I can hear every note Stephanie's computer is sending out. They're all perfect. The code is exactly right."

Madeline lifted an eyebrow. "It's good to know that you can tell."

L. M. grinned.

Meanwhile, Jean had turned the plane around, and disappeared from the Antarctica monitor. Moments later, she shot out above the landing strip. She circled the plane a couple of times to reduce speed, then landed without a problem and taxied to the underground hangar.

Madeline straightened up and waved at the others. "Okay, let's go meet her." She put a hand on Jay's shoulder. "Sorry, Jay, you need to stay here."

Jay smiled. "No problem!"

Brittany raised a hand. "Party tonight, our place!"

"Champagne and sparkling grape juice!" Sumita added.

The next morning, Irene walked with Jay to the staff meeting. "That was a fun party last night."

Jay nodded. "It was. I had no idea there was a croquet course in the back of the residence."

"Yes, it's nice to play under the stars, with the lights. There's a mini-golf course in the basement of the residence, too."

"I ought to try that out some time."

After everyone was seated, Madeline turned to Yolanda. "You said you had something, Yolanda?"

"Yes." She turned to take in each of her colleagues before she continued. "I've been tracking Charles's expenditures. I believe that he is constructing an army of simulacrums."

Chapter 7

Jay's mouth flew open in a grin. "We can track his money? I'm all for it, but...will it get us into any trouble?"

Madeline turned to him. "I was an attorney when I was in the service. Everything this company does is legal and above board. If we need to do something...irregular, we purchased a small island in the Caribbean in international waters and anything that has its origin there, such as gathering information, is untouchable by any jurisdiction."

"Of course Charles has no such scruples," L. M. said.

Jay nodded.

Yolanda turned from Jay to Madeline. "He's opened a factory on the east coast. The raw material purchases he's made, the machinery he's bought, the contracts he's signed, all point to the mass-production of simulacrums."

"To be used against us, presumably," Athena said.

"Possibly," Madeline said. "We can't say we didn't see it coming."

Jay looked to Terry. "Do we have any defenses against them?"

"Hell, yes," L. M. said before Terry could open her mouth. "We have an arsenal of weed-killers."

"He wants Arachne and he wants it bad," Stephanie said.

Madeline leaned back in her chair. "Well, he's not going to get it. Next order of business." She turned to Ginnie Mae. "Ginnie Mae, you wanted to bring something up?"

"Yes. If we're going to use Arachne for defense, I think we ought to see if we can fire a gun from inside it."

"Why would we ever want to do that?" Sumita said.

"That's not the point," Daphne said. "A lot of devices have catastrophically failed because the inventor thought 'that will never happen' and never tested the possibility. We have to know what Arachne does if that happens, even if we never do it."

Madeline turned to Stephanie. "Stephanie?"

Stephanie blew out a breath. "Daphne's right. It hadn't occurred to me that Arachne could ever be used that way, but since it could, we have to know."

"All right, let's test it," Madeline said.

"Arachne isn't going to like it," L. M. chanted.

Daphne put her head down on the table briefly and sighed heavily as she raised it again.

Madeline ignored that and turned to L. M. "What do you mean?"

"Percussion."

"Percussion?" Stephanie echoed. "But music has percussion. The motors on the vehicles we sent through had percussion. Why would percussion bother Arachne?"

"Discord, then," L. M. said. "I don't know all those fancy scientific words. But if you can't tell the difference between a gunshot and a melody, I can't help you."

"What about the 1812 Overture? With cannon?" Stephanie challenged.

L. M. tapped the table. "Every time we've tested Arachne with music, the melody has been in tune. Even an engine has a rhythm: chuga-chuga, chuga-chuga. Put a random explosion in there, which is what a gunshot is, and you'll throw it off."

Stephanie spread her hands. "How can you possibly know that? Arachne is an electronic device, and is controlled by electrical impulses."

L. M. shook her head. "Wrong. It's a musical instrument and has to be treated as such." At Stephanie's skeptical look, L. M. added, "Well, how far did you get before Jay discovered Arachne can carry a tune, hm?"

Madeline waved a hand. "Daphne's right. We have to know what Arachne will do. Ginnie Mae can get a rifle and test it out. Daphne, you go with her, since Ginnie Mae isn't trained on Arachne."

"Why not me?" Stephanie protested.

"Because if something goes wrong, I want you here." Madeline turned to L. M. "And if anything goes wrong, I want you in there with them, L. M."

L. M. grinned, rolled her shoulders, and pushed away from the table. "No problem. It's my job to save your butts."

Once again, at the test, Jay sat at his desk as the others stood behind the blast shield in front of Arachne. His cave complex monitor showed L. M. talking into her cell phone.

"Has the estate been evacuated, Aunt Thelma?"

A voice came through the phone speaker, amplified by the monitor. "Everyone and every animal is below ground. I set up the wall of hay bales with a bull's eye painted on it right where you said."

"Thanks, Aunt Thelma. I'll tell you when it's all clear."

"Roger that."

L. M. pocketed the phone. She turned to Daphne at her right, and Ginnie Mae at her left. Ginnie Mae carried the high-powered rifle with the telescopic sight. "Ready? Let's go."

Jay could see Stephanie at her laptop. She sent out the tone. The three women walked in and disappeared.

For about half a minute, nothing happened. Arachne hummed and lit up as it usually did.

"*POP!*"

The percussion caused everyone to jump. Arachne went dark as if someone had turned off a light switch. It stood there, silent.

Vivian glared at Stephanie. "You killed it! You killed Arachne!"

"Everyone just stay calm." Madeline turned to Stephanie, who sent out an array of tones.

Arachne did not respond.

Madeline spoke into the intercom. "Jay, can you get the Yeager estate on your monitor?"

"Doing it," Jay said. "I see the hay bales and the target painted on them, but there's no one there."

Meanwhile, Stephanie continued to work her laptop. She tried tone after tone; nothing worked. Next to her, Nadia tried other sequences from the other laptop; still no response.

Jay spoke into the intercom. "You know, when Stephanie first activated Arachne, there was a song that sort of reminded me of a Sousa tune."

"Yeah, I thought the same thing," Nadia said.

"Do you have anything by Sousa in your database?" he asked.

"Yes, there has to be...," Nadia said.

"Worth a try," Stephanie added, looking over at Nadia's screen.

Arachne sprang to life, singing brightly with multicolored lights at its edges.

Nadia leaned back slightly. "Symphony's song identification routine says it's playing 'Good Morning Starshine.'"

"It doesn't sound like that," Vivian protested.

Jay shook his head. The tune Arachne sang did not sound that way to him, either.

"Well, I'm going with the computer." Yolanda began to sing. The rest of the staff who were in the company choir joined in with her.

Seconds later, L. M. stepped out of Arachne, smile on her face, toothpick in her mouth, rifle slung over a shoulder. One hand held Ginnie Mae's. The other held Daphne's. Ginnie Mae wept uncontrollably. Daphne appeared stunned.

"Butts saved," L. M. announced.

Brittany ran forward and enveloped Ginnie Mae. Sumita grabbed a chair, set it in front of Daphne, and eased Daphne into it.

Brittany patted Ginnie Mae's back. "It's all right, Ginnie Mae, it's all right."

"She's o-kay," L. M. drawled. "Haven't you heard of tears of happiness before?"

Ginnie Mae did not respond, but she managed to nod her head.

Sumita knelt next to Daphne. "You okay, Daphne?"

She shook her head. "I'm not religious, but that was as near a religious experience as I have ever had."

Brittany, still soothing Ginnie Mae, turned to Daphne. "You don't have to be religious to have a transcendental experience."

Daphne waved a hand. "Yeah, that's what I must have had, all right."

Madeline turned to L. M. "Maybe you can lose the toothpick and tell us what happened."

L. M. took the toothpick out of her mouth and grinned. "Sure. We got in there, Ginnie Mae knelt and took aim at the hay bale target, and shot."

"Everything went black," Daphne said.

L. M.'s smile was undiminished. "Couldn't see a thing. So I took a deep breath and sang...."

Through the monitor at his desk, Jay saw L. M. raise her arms and start to sing, "Good Morning, Starshine," and Arachne lit up behind her. He had heard her sing with the rest, and alone briefly, but not all out this way before. His eyebrows went up. L. M. should be singing at the Met, he thought.

After a few bars, L. M. put her arms down. "Arachne didn't do anything at first. But I kept singing, and then above us, there was a light. Soon we could see everything, as before."

"Then Arachne sang back," Daphne said.

"It sounded like angels," Ginnie Mae said.

"It sounded like voices," Daphne said.

"What where they saying?" Yolanda asked.

"Nothing," L. M. said. "It was like an action scene in a movie, where they have a chorus in the background singing 'aaahhhh' and such."

"Did you see anyone else?" Madeline said.

"No, it was Arachne, I told you," L. M. waved at the laptops in front of Stephanie and Nadia. "You get your computers to mimic human voices all the time. Arachne can, too."

"There was something else about it, though," Daphne said, "something magnificent, but I can't quite put my finger on it."

"Arachne increases your endorphin level, we know that," Sumita said. "That could account for the feeling."

"It was like Arachne was alive, somehow, and communicating with us, telling us everything would be all right." Daphne shrugged. "I know that's not scientific, but...."

"I felt it, too," Ginnie Mae said.

Daphne turned to Madeline. "Madeline, there is no way that Charles is ever going to get his hands on Arachne. He'll have to shoot through me, first."

Madeline stepped forward and put a hand on Daphne's arm. "I am absolutely determined to see that he never gets it."

"Well, now that's settled...." L. M. took out her smartphone. "Aunt Thelma, all clear. You can come out now."

"Roger that. I was watching the target through the binoculars. Your shooter hit the bull's eye. Clean shot. The bullet's probably embedded in the block of wood we put behind the hay bales."

"Got it. Talk to you later." L. M. put the phone away and grinned. "Test over."

At the next staff meeting, after Madeline settled in her chair, Stephanie said, "Before we get started, I want to say something."

Madeline turned to her. "Be my guest."

Stephanie turned to each of them in turn. "There's nothing mystical about Arachne. I designed it. Athena, Ginnie Mae, Terry, and I built it. I rechecked all the mechanics after yesterday's test. There's nothing different. It's just a device. An incredible device, if I may say so myself, but a device. That's all."

L. M. leaned toward Stephanie. "The sum is greater than the parts."

Madeline held up a hand to forestall further debate. "It is what it is, and whatever it is, we're its guardian now. Each of you can think of it as you will; the question is, how are we going to use it?" She turned to Jay. "Jay, have you plumbed the depth of our satellite and remote communication systems yet?"

"In what way?"

"Can you monitor air traffic control, 911 calls, police bands, things like that?"

"Oh, yes, ma'am...Madeline."

"Good. Keep an eye on them, and keep watching the 24-hour news channels and monitoring the social media. If you see anything, notify me and I'll make the call."

"Do you mean we're going to go and rescue people?" Irene said excitedly.

Madeline smiled at her. "Yes, Irene, that's what it means."

She clapped her hands. "Good."

"I presume," Madeline continued, "you've all been making progress on your respective tasks. Ginnie Mae, I want you to build a set of changing booths near Arachne, one for each of us, with a name plate on each one."

"Doors or curtains?" Ginnie Mae asked.

"I think curtains will do, unless anyone has an objection?" Madeline paused a moment, and when no one spoke, she continued, "Put the masks, helmets, boots, whatever, in the booths when you're done with them."

"I'll set up a portable medical cart in the event we're doing an ambulance run," Sumita said.

Madeline nodded at her. "Good idea. Now, as for team leaders, the chain of command is as follows: me, then Jean, Stephanie, Athena, Nadia, Terry, Daphne, Brittany, Sumita, and L. M." She turned to L. M. "And so help me, if I see you with a toothpick in your mouth on location, I'll fire you."

L. M. grinned. "Got it."

"Anyone have any questions or comments on the chain of command?" Madeline asked.

There were a few seconds of silence before Daphne said, "Who cares, as long as we get to go?"

Jay heard murmurs of assent.

Madeline smiled. "Good."

The first few weeks after he had moved into the residence, Jay kept mostly to himself, recovering from the trauma of having his medication withdrawn from him, and settling in to a new environment. Gradually, he began to learn the patterns of his new surroundings and socialize more with his co-workers. One day, after work, Yolanda asked if he played bridge or would be willing to learn. When he politely declined, saying that bridge was not his game, Yolanda directed him to an electronic bulletin board within the residence showing him how to sign up for other games or post that he was looking for players for a particular game. He found that Stephanie, Athena, Nadia, and Daphne, for instance, met on most Wednesday nights for a multi-player space exploration game. One night, he joined them and had a rip-roaring good time.

On the last weekend of the regular season, Ginnie Mae asked if he wanted to go to the baseball game on Friday night. He accepted and offered to drive, since the idea of riding in back of Ginnie Mae's motorcycle was not appealing to him. They agreed to meet in the underground parking lot after work. As he walked to his car, he saw a number of his co-workers get into their cars and drive off. As he stood there, watching, he heard a voice behind him.

"Need a map to get out of the garage?" L. M. asked.

He turned. "Uh, no.... I'm surprised to see so many people leaving the residence with Charles's spies all around."

She touched the toothpick in her mouth. "Who do you want running your life, Charles or you?"

Surprised by the question, he paused before answering. "Um. Me, of course."

"If you hide out here because you're afraid of Charles, that's letting him run your life. We ain't going to do that, and neither are you, from the look of it."

"Well, yeah, Ginnie Mae and I are going to a baseball game, but we're going to keep an eye out, and I have everyone's number in case there's trouble."

L. M. nodded. "That's what everyone else is doing, too. Besides, Charles's agents aren't as tough as they think they are. We can take 'em."

Ginnie Mae walked up. "Ready to go?"

He turned to her. "Uh, sure." When he swung back to say good-bye to L. M., he saw that she had already walked away.

When they got inside the ballpark, they headed to the concession stand. Jay watched to verify the beer vendor filled his cup from the same spigot as everyone else, and the hot dog man picked his randomly from the vat. Ginnie Mae also seemed to note carefully that her food came from common origins.

As they walked to their seats, they ran into Don. "Hey, buddy, it's been a while."

Jay gestured to Ginnie Mae. "Ginnie Mae, this is Don. We used to work together. Don, Ginnie Mae works with me."

Ginnie Mae returned a polite smile and nod.

Don nodded back. "Say, I have a friend who has a corporate suite overlooking home plate and it's nearly empty. Care to join us?"

Ginnie Mae shook her head, and Jay said, "No, thanks. We have seats along the first baseline and prefer to be outdoors."

"Suit yourself. Enjoy the game." Don walked away.

The home team won the game. They had enjoyed a winning record that season, but they were not destined for the playoffs.

Still, he and Ginnie Mae agreed that they seemed to have good potential for the next season.

As they were driving back, windows down and enjoying the after-sunset breeze, Jay asked, "Can you tell where Charles's spies are?"

Ginnie Mae shook her head. "I don't have as sharp an eye on that as Madeline or L. M. do. But someone probably saw us go and come back."

"Yeah. I can't tell, either."

When the residence and company headquarters were in sight—softly illuminated in the evening—the car's headlights showed someone on a horse approaching the road.

"That's Terry," Ginnie Mae said.

Jay stopped. Terry waved at them as she crossed in front of them. When she was safely away, Jay drove forward again. "I didn't see a stable at the residence."

"Our next-door neighbors on the other side of the bluff run a horse ranch. L. M. checked them out. They're okay. It's a retired couple—Ramona and Luis Santana—who bought the ranch three years before we built company headquarters here."

"Have you been with Madeline since the beginning?"

"Almost. It was just Madeline, Yolanda, Terry, and L. M. at first."

"How did you join the company?"

"Same as you. Madeline hired people that she knew from the service, or people referred to her by people she knew from the service. One of my brothers worked for her when he was in the army and told her I was a good mechanic. We were in a rented building in the city then." When they reached the parking lot, Ginnie Mae pointed. "Stop here. Let me show you something."

Curious, Jay parked the car. He got out when Ginnie Mae did.

Ginnie Mae pointed upward, to the rock face that headquarters had been built into. "Madeline put in a lot of stuff that we don't use anymore...or never used. Terry called it 'planned redundancy.' What you see up there that looks like a hole in the rock is actually a sentry tower. Only Irene and I go up there now. On weekends, sometimes we get up before everyone—except Madeline, she gets up before anyone else–and do target practice from there."

In the dimness, Jay could just make out the feature. "You mean you shoot things from up there? What is it that you shoot?"

Ginnie Mae chuckled. "Oh, not guns. Madeline had Terry and I make up a projectile thrower. It's sort of a catapult but not exactly. Anyway, L. M. said we had defenses much better than that, so we never used it. It's up there in the sentry tower and Irene and I can slide it out. We chalk a target in the sand next to the parking lot and throw rocks at it. We have to clean it up before anyone sees so there's not a mess."

Jay turned to Ginnie Mae. "I take it the sentry tower was abandoned when the monitors were put in?"

Ginnie Mae looked back at him. "Oh, the sentry tower is there in case the monitors go out...which they don't, but it's part of the planned redundancy they talk about." She opened the car door and got back inside. As Jay opened the driver's side door, he saw Jean's car pass the parking lot and continue to the entrance of the underground garage. He followed her in and parked at his designated place. As he and Ginnie Mae walked to the door to the residence, he saw Nadia driving in. When they reached the residence, he saw Athena and Irene in the hallway, headed toward the mini-golf course.

"Lots of activity on a Friday night," he said to Ginnie Mae.

"Oh, that happens all weekend. If you get out of your room, you'll see."

Jay had been keeping his curtains closed most of the time, but the next morning he opened them. He also activated the monitor in his apartment. Each apartment had a monitor overlooking the outside parking lot and the underground garage so that residents could look in on their cars if they wished. Sipping his after-breakfast coffee, he saw Vivian loading a bag of golf clubs in a car trunk before driving off. L. M. hauled her harp in the back of an SUV, followed by Stephanie sticking in her keyboard. Nadia climbed into the passenger side, carrying a case that appeared to be for a flute or clarinet.

Encouraged by their boldness, Jay decided to go shopping. Even though the residence did have its own supplies, these were mostly limited to the basic necessities, and Jay thought he could do with a few more items. He drove into town, and after purchasing some nonperishable snacks, went to a large warehouse store to check out the latest gadgets. As he looked around, he noticed a brown-haired man standing near him. He wore a short-sleeved shirt, knee-length khaki pants, gray socks, walking shoes, and sunglasses. Out in the desert as he was, it was not unusual for him to see men wearing dark glasses—he wore them himself when driving on sunny days. But he usually took them off indoors. Still, he mused, some people wore sunglasses indoors...not that unusual. When Jay went from one section to the other, he noticed the man would also change sections, though keeping a respectful distance. Curious, Jay moved towards the man, only to see the man casually walk away to somewhere else. Keeping the man in view, he saw the man pick up things, appear to examine them, and replace them on the shelves.

Suddenly, a youngster running through the store bumped into the man, followed by another youngster racing after him who also collided with the man. He lost his balance; the boys sprinted on. No one but Jay saw the man's head turn around a little too far, the arms and legs flex as if they were rubber tubing, and the sunglasses temporarily slip down to where Jay caught a glimpse of the eyes. The form regained its balance, adjusted the sunglasses, and stood, taking on a more natural, human pose, and continued casually picking up things and putting them back.

Jay tuned away and grinned as he sauntered to the checkout counter. After paying for his memory cards and walking away, he muttered under his breath, "I made you, you asshole."

He drove home in an upbeat mood, but checked his rear view mirror periodically for sign of pursuit. There was none. He parked the car in the garage and entered the residence. The door to the archery room was open. Yolanda pulled back an arrow while Jean held her own bow and arrow loosely beside her. After Yolanda shot, hitting the bull's eye, Jay stepped in and held out his arms triumphantly.

"I've seen a simulacrum!" he announced happily.

Yolanda looked up. "Did it follow you home?"

Jay put his arms down. "No, I checked."

"Good." Jean pulled back her bow, shot, then faced Jay again. "Congratulations. Once you've noticed them, you'll be able to identify them more easily in the future."

Chapter 8

In the days since their last test, Jay had almost forgotten about Arachne when his surveillance computer sounded an alarm. Great Pacific Airlines flight 112 had dropped out of radar. Immediately, he aimed one of their satellites in that direction and saw a large passenger plane with smoke issuing from it. He hit the panic button to Madeline's office.

Madeline appeared from the stairway. "Nadia saw it, too, and alerted me. Stay here and monitor the situation while Nadia and Stephanie control Arachne." She ran to the cave entrance without waiting for a response.

Jay turned to the cave complex monitor. Jean emerged from one of the booths that Ginnie Mae had set up, wearing uniform, helmet, and goggles, and raced to the hangar.

Madeline's voice came over the intercom. "Jay, have they issued a mayday?"

Jay checked his communications panel. "No. Denver air traffic control is trying to raise them, without success."

Jean's filtered voice came through. "The plane...are they trying to turn around?"

"No," Jay and Nadia said at the same time.

"Nadia, help Stephanie. Let Jay take over the surveillance data."

"Right, Madeline."

Stephanie said, "Nadia, I'll do the directional coordinates. You do the musical translation."

"Will do," Nadia said.

"How far from Denver are they?" Jean asked Jay.

"About 200 miles southwest. Destination was to be San Diego, according to the airline's schedule," Jay said.

"Speed?"

"About 450 mph, and slowing gradually."

"Good, 'slowing' means someone's probably at the controls. Ascending or descending?"

"Descending."

"That's bad. Most pilots would fly up if there were a fire to try to put it out. If they haven't, it may mean they can't."

Jay watched as Jean guided the plane out of the hangar and onto the runway. She revved up the engines and took off.

"Jean," he heard Athena say over the communications system, "activate the concealment system *now*."

"Done."

Jay saw the plane turn into a blur as the concealment system bent the light around it.

"Jean," Stephanie said. "Arachne should put you right above the plane. Go."

Jay watched as the blur disappeared...and reappeared above the plane.

"Okay, I can see the plane. Flying around it. I can't see passengers through the windows. I don't know if that means they've asked them to put their heads down in preparation to attempt a landing or if they're dead. I see the pilots, though. They're working the controls. There's fire coming from beneath the plane near the cargo hatch. Part of the side is burning, too. Engines seem to be all right but they're going down fast. Stephanie, you have to put a portal ahead of the plane, let them fly into it, and put them down somewhere."

"Where?" Stephanie asked.

"On it." Jay turned another satellite to Denver, but any place he saw to land a plane was occupied.

"Jay, we haven't got all day," Jean said. "That plane has to land, and fast."

"Okay, okay." Jay remembered a television program that often filmed at a deserted runway in Alameda, California. He turned the satellite there and saw that today, at least, they were not filming...the place was deserted. As he worked, he heard voices over the intercom.

"Tell the pilot to lower the landing gear," Madeline said.

"Can't make radio contact. Tried," Jean said.

"This plane's design has a digital screen in the cockpit, and so do you," Athena said. "Type it in. Essentially, you're texting them."

"Sent!" After a brief pause, Jean added, "They're doing it!"

Meanwhile, Jay had determined the GPS coordinates of the landing field.

"Now, Jay! Now, now, now!" Jean called.

"Sending Stephanie the GPS coordinates...now."

"Stephanie!" Jean called.

"It takes a second or two to align the portal!"

"We don't have a second; it's going to crash into the mountains!"

"We got it!" Nadia said.

Arachne's tune crescendoed.

The plane appeared over the deserted airfield. Jay held his breath as the plane's wheels hit the runway. Would the airbrakes work? They had been slowing as they were descending, but they still had been going pretty fast. Maybe going through Arachne had reduced the airspeed? No, it tended to make them go fast, but wait...Stephanie said she had been able to compensate for that. In any case, the plane seemed to be slowing. The only problem now was, did they have enough runway? Jay found himself clenching his fists as if pulling on the reins of a horse, willing them to stop. Finally, they did, with mere yards to spare. Then there was an awful second when nothing happened. Flames still licked the undercarriage of the plane. Jay feared it had been all for nothing.

The doors popped open and the emergency slides deployed. Passengers slid out and ran from the plane when they hit the tarmac, away from the flames.

Jay heard cheering behind him. He had not noticed that Yolanda, Vivian, and Irene had been looking over his shoulder. Cheers came from the cave complex, as well.

"Jean, where are you?" Madeline said.

"I'm over the plane. The passengers have escaped. I'm going to dump some foam over the fuselage."

"Okay, go ahead," Madeline said. "They know something's going on, and all I can see on the monitor is a blur where you are."

"Oh, my gosh," Jay said, realizing that he needed to contact local emergency services. He tapped into the Alameda 911 system, only to find that passengers with cell phones were already calling for help.

On the monitor, foam fell from the sky. It kept the fire from spreading, but did not completely put it out.

"Jean, we need to bring you home," Stephanie said.

"Okay, circling over the plane."

Within a minute, the blur that was the company plane disappeared over Alameda and reappeared over the company runway. The blur quickly formed into the shape of the plane as Jean landed.

Yolanda patted Jay's shoulder. "Good job, Jay."

Jay let out a breath and ran a hand through his hair. "Thanks."

Once the plane was in the hangar, Jay could see Jean scramble down the stairway, race across the cave complex, grab Stephanie, and embrace her in a tight hug. "Thank you, thank you, thank you."

"It worked," Stephanie said. She sounded pleasantly surprised.

When Jean released Stephanie, she hugged Nadia, then Madeline, then Athena. She waved at one of the cave monitors. "Thank you, Jay."

"You're welcome," he called into the intercom.

Brittany walked up to the group. "We all need to decompress. Jean, Athena, do your usual post-flight checks. Jean, get out of the uniform and into something more comfortable. We'll have a popcorn party."

Within an hour, they were all gathered in the large open area between Jay's desk and Yolanda's and Vivian's offices. Zoe had brought blankets and large pillows from the residence. They sat or reclined on them, watching the cable news. Each had a container of popcorn and a drink at their side.

By this time, the press had arrived and a reporter was interviewing a disheveled passenger.

"I thought we were goners," said the man. "We could see fire outside. The cabin was getting stuffy. The plane was going down, fast. The flight attendants said to put our heads down and prepare for a rough landing, but someone must have had their head up because someone said they saw this blur... said maybe it was a UFO. Then we heard music, and we were here."

"Everyone I've talked to has mentioned the music," the reporter said.

"Yeah, it was just for a few seconds, between being there and being here. But it was definitely music."

"Someone must have got it on their cell phone," Yolanda said.

"Probably haven't run into that person yet," Daphne said.

"Well, they already found someone who photographed Jean," Vivian said.

Nadia threw her head back to look at Jean. "The blurry UFO."

Jean smiled and turned to Athena. "Worked just as designed."

Athena picked up another handful of popcorn. "And radar didn't detect you, either."

"Shh," Irene said. "They're interviewing a pilot."

A woman in a pilot's uniform appeared on the screen. "There's no doubt in my mind we were headed for a crash. We had no control. The engines worked, but there was no way to steer, and we couldn't get the nose up. We were losing altitude fast."

"Did you get any communication from the UFO?"

"Yes. Our digital dashboard lit up and the message said to lower our landing gear. We felt we had nothing to lose, so we did."

"Was it in English?"

"Yes."

"Any other message?"

"No."

"Did you hear the music?"

"Yes. After we lowered the landing gear, the sky disappeared and for a second or two it seemed we were in a building with a high vaulted ceiling. I heard music in the background. Then we were on the runway here."

"What sort of music was it? Was the tune familiar?"

The pilot shook her head. "Nothing I can recall hearing before. It was pleasant music, that's all I can say."

Terry took a sip from her can of root beer. "Well, Charles now knows what Arachne is and what it can do."

"He probably already had a good idea," Madeline said.

L. M. grinned. "Yeah. And he's probably throwing a temper tantrum because he doesn't have it."

"Won't he try to redouble his efforts to get it?" Jay said.

"Sure he will," L. M. said.

"He will," Madeline affirmed, "but he's not getting it."

"Over my dead body," Daphne said.

Meanwhile, the reporter had faced the camera. "Our news organization would like to extend an invitation to the party or parties responsible for an interview...anytime, anyplace."

"Ain't happening," L. M. said.

Yolanda turned to Madeline. "Something just occurred to me, Madeline. Now that Charles knows that Arachne is active, won't he try to stage a disaster to draw us out and try to get into Arachne?"

Madeline sighed. "Yes, there was always that risk."

Vivian turned in their direction. "Well, forget Charles...any clown out there might try to stage a disaster just to get our picture!"

"Ain't gettin' that, either," L. M. said. "Unless they have a helmet, goggles, and mask fetish."

"It's inevitable that someday we'll be in a situation where we'll be leaving DNA behind," Sumita said.

Madeline took a breath, then nodded. "That's a more calculated risk, but yes, that could happen. But we'll cross that bridge when we come to it."

On the screen, the reporter was interviewing a police officer. "So you say that if the party or parties responsible come forward, they won't face any charges?"

The officer shook his head. "Congress passed a law last year protecting civilians giving aid in a disaster. It's called the 'no harm, no foul' law, and as long as it's obvious the civilian is trying to help, there are no charges."

Athena turned to Madeline. "Can anyone trace that law back to you?"

Madeline shook her head. "There were plenty of volunteer organizations willing to lobby for it. Nothing can be attributed particularly to me."

Jay glanced out the window and stood. "Delivery truck."

L. M. stood and looked out. "Sam's Flowers. They were on my beat when I was a cop."

The truck stopped and a delivery man came out, carrying flowers.

"That's Sam. He's okay," L. M. said.

Athena stepped up to Jay's console. "Let's scan him anyway." She adjusted some controls, and a readout came on a screen as Sam walked in the outer entrance. "He's clean, and the flowers are too."

"Radiation?" Jay asked. He was surprised that he had not discovered that feature before. But he had watched Athena carefully and was confident he could duplicate the effort.

"Nothing harmful." Athena turned to Jay. "New feature. Sorry; I was going to tell you and got wrapped up in other things."

"No problem." Jay opened the inner door and Sam came though.

"Delivery," Sam announced.

Madeline stepped forward, took the flowers, and tipped Sam.

"Thank you," Sam said. He nodded to Madeline and then to L. M. before leaving.

"Hydrangeas. Nice," Irene said.

"Is there a card?" Vivian asked.

"Yes." Madeline took it out and read it. "'Congratulations, ladies...'" She glanced at Jay. "'..and gentleman. Charles Vance.'" She put the flower vase on the counter.

L. M. laughed out loud. "Well, ain't he sweet."

"He's not going to rat us out, is he?" Vivian asked.

"Hell, no," L. M. said. "Not as long as he still thinks he's going to get Arachne and have it all to himself."

Jay turned on the news in his apartment as soon as he got out of bed. He knew from watching reports on previous incidents that more detailed information generally came in the next day. And it did: he was relieved to hear there were no deaths, though there were some hospitalizations. That was the most important item. As more time passed, the reporters added that the preliminary cause of the fire was an e-cigarette packed in luggage that had accidentally ignited. The plane and investigators still lingered at the site. Reporters interviewed the crew of the television show that routinely used the deserted runway for filming, and they denied being the cause. They added they would love to interview the responsible parties, as well.

A person-on-the-street reporter gathered several opinions. One said that this was a sign of first contact with interplanetary travelers. Another said it was a sign of angels visiting Earth. Still another speculated it was a top-secret government project (earlier, Jay heard the White House press secretary deny that possibility).

The panel of scientists proved to be more interesting. They agreed that someone had made a groundbreaking discovery but had not published it. Opinions differed on whether the unknown scientist should make the discovery public. The scientists were also asked about "the blur" and said there had to be some sort of light-bending technology going on. They added that the evasion of radar was well within current engineering capabilities.

The news channel showed "the blur" several times. They also found someone whose camera had been running during the transfer through Arachne and had picked up the music. Reporters interviewed professors of music theory who shrugged their shoulders and said they heard nothing special. As one put it, "Mozart it ain't."

At the staff meeting that morning, Yolanda distributed envelopes.

"Bonuses for everyone for a job well done," Madeline said.

Each person peeked into their envelope and extended thanks.

Jay turned to Stephanie. "The news broadcasted the tones within Arachne this morning. Is there any chance Charles or someone else could reverse-engineer Arachne?"

Stephanie shook her head. "The tones are nothing without the mechanism behind it. Besides, remember that in the very beginning, we worked Arachne without using any music whatsoever."

"It's just that the music allows more sophisticated operations," Nadia added.

"Good." Jay took a breath. "Because it's getting coverage 24/7 right now."

"The news cycle is certain to turn to something else soon," Madeline said. "It's the end of the Supreme Court session, the U. N. General Assembly will convene shortly...."

"...The World Series will start," Ginnie Mae added.

"...Then there's Halloween!" Irene said.

"Some spoiled celebrity will jump into a fountain naked and then they'll talk about that," Vivian said. "Speaking of Halloween, though, if anyone wants me to make their costume for the Yeagers' Halloween party, let me know now so I can get it done in time."

L. M. turned to Jay. "Forgot to mention, Jay, that the family throws a Halloween party every year. It's free and open to the public, and you can come, too."

Jay smiled. "I'd be happy to."

Chapter 9

Vivian fitted Jay's Halloween costume in her office. He stood in front of a mirror to see the effect. After telling her that he wanted to be Robin Hood, Vivian had put together an approximation of a period outfit, with a shirt, tunic over the shirt, leggings, leather belt, and boots. Since the Yeagers did not allow real weapons, the quiver had wooden dowels with feathers on one end. He slung the imitation bow over a shoulder. Turning away from the mirror, he bowed to thank her. Then he walked out toward the cave complex, passing Zoe as he did so.

Though they could have used Arachne to get to the Yeager estate, Madeline said it was better if they took the company jet. Athena volunteered to remain behind to mind Arachne in case of emergency; Irene explained to Jay that to Athena, Halloween was just another day. Daphne had gone to a Halloween party in town.

Jay made straight for the hangar, where he saw Jean already at the plane, dressed as a knight from a faraway galaxy of long ago. She even had a transparent rod fastened to the end of a handle, which glowed and hummed as she swung it around. Madeline and L. M. conversed softly nearby. Madeline wore an astronaut's outfit with the helmet faceplate pushed back. L. M. had dressed as a 19th century sailing ship captain.

When Jay neared them, L. M. called out, "Don't smash the jack o'lanterns. They're expensive porcelain. If you want to take out your aggressions, there's a pumpkin-carving station with real pumpkins."

Jay chuckled. "Don't worry, I'm current with my meds."

L. M. nodded and turned back to Madeline. Jay continued toward Irene, who wore a pink tutu, pink tights, pink ballet slippers, and a tiara on her head.

"Nice outfit," he said. "Everything looks real pretty, especially the tiara."

She smiled and touched it briefly. "Yes, I had it made special at the jewelers."

He raised his eyebrows. "Are those real diamonds?"

"Sure they are. I had lots of money left over when I had worked here for awhile, even after I put money in savings and retirement, so I bought this."

Jay nodded. "Well, it looks lovely."

"Thank you."

Sumita and Brittany walked up. Both wore pantsuits. Sumita had a brown jacket, green hat, and multi-colored scarf. Brittany's jacket was tan, with what appeared to be a stalk of celery as a corsage.

They smiled. "We're Doctors," Sumita explained.

"She's number four, and I'm number five," Brittany clarified.

Stephanie and Nadia walked up behind them. Nadia wore a green hijab, a green mask, a green body suit with a lantern in the middle of the chest, and a ring on her finger with a lantern symbol. Stephanie had on a uniform from the literary school of witchcraft and wizardry.

"I presume that pipe is empty," Madeline called.

Jay turned to see a costumed figure wearing black pants and shoes, a plaid capelet and matching deerstalker hat. The figure pulled out the pipe. "Of course, my dear Madeline."

Madeline smiled and turned back to L. M.

Jay approached the figure. "Terry?"

The figure nodded.

"Wow, that's impressive."

"Thanks."

Zoe walked by, dressed in a brown bear costume.

Jay turned to Terry. "Lots of interesting outfits."

"Wait until you see Vivian," Terry said.

Ginnie Mae walked up, wearing an empire dress from the Regency period, looking like a character from a Jane Austen novel. She wore a wide-brimmed hat with a pink band and carried a matching parasol.

"If Vivian doesn't get here soon, we're taking off without her," Madeline said.

"There she is," Jean called.

Vivian would have been difficult to miss, wearing an elaborate Renaissance Elizabethan gown. She could have been a duchess in the royal court, going to dance with Sir Walter Raleigh and Sir Francis Drake. Yolanda accompanied her, wearing a captain's uniform from the second Trek series.

The flight to the Yeager estate took less than an hour. L. M. led the way from the airstrip to a low building. Jay offered an arm to Vivian and Ginnie Mae, wondering if they would take one; both did.

They descended a wide ramp to a set of glass doors flanked by glass panels—though Jay suspected they were similar to, if not the same as, the protective transparencies on the company headquarters. Lighted jack o'lanterns had been spread around—Jay noticed that they were indeed made of porcelain, painted orange. Once inside, they descended another ramp to a level the size of a commercial airline hangar. Vivian and Ginnie Mae let go of his arms and began to mingle.

Most went to the refreshment table first. There was no hard liquor, but there was punch, apple cider, and ice cream on sticks or in paper cups, all orange-colored. L. M. greeted her Uncle Zach, who wore a Revolutionary War uniform. Next to him stood a formidable-looking couple filling cups with punch. They were dressed as football players, wearing generic uniforms complete with pads and helmets. L. M. addressed them as Aunt Thelma and Uncle Ned. Jay accepted the punch graciously and noticed, as they handed out cups, their matching "Semper Fi" tattoos.

A couple stood at the pumpkin-carving stand, helping young and old carvers as they worked. They were dressed as elves. L. M. hugged them and called them "Dad" and "Mom." He could certainly see the resemblance; they were all tall, broad-shouldered, and solidly built. Someone addressed "Dad" as "Phil" and another addressed "Mom" as "Carol."

There was no lack of things to do. In a corner, a television screen had been set up, showing Halloween-related cartoons. An interested audience of mostly, but not entirely, younger viewers had gathered, sitting on the soft area rug. Zoe had wandered in that direction; toddlers ran up to her and hugged her legs. She reached down and patted their shoulders.

Another area had a large monitor set up. Jay could see it was a large, interactive video game, where participants, by moving in front of the screen, could capture passing ghosts for points. Elsewhere, a sort of bowling alley had been setup, with pumpkin-shaped bowling balls. Instead of pins, tall and narrow plastic cylinders with ghosts painted on them had been arranged to knock over. A shallow tank filled with water held apples, but instead of bobbing for them, guests of all ages used long-handled scoops to try to snag them. There was also plenty of free space for people to simply mingle, talk, and admire each other's costumes.

As the night wore on, L. M.'s parents picked up their violins and Terry, still wearing the Sherlock Holmes costume, instructed anyone interested in a country line dance. Jay and Ginnie Mae were two of many who participated.

At the end of the evening, Thelma and Ned announced fireworks, so everyone made their way outside and sat on the grass or in the sand to watch. Once the fireworks were over, they thanked their hosts and Jean flew them back home.

In early November, an ice storm hit the Austin metro area during the evening rush hour. While Jay monitored the 911 calls, wondering if he should sound an alarm, Athena walked up to his station.

"I need a satellite view of the freeway system," she said.

Jay leaned over the controls. "I can't, due to the clouds, but I can tap into the traffic cameras."

While Athena examined the screens, Madeline appeared from the stairway and walked over.

Athena looked up. "Madeline, I want to deploy Stacy, and be in charge of this one."

Madeline nodded. "Go ahead."

Jay turned to Madeline and Athena. "The traffic is gridlocked. Streets and freeways are filled with cars going nowhere. Emergency responders can't come through."

Athena tapped Jay's screen. "Send this to Stephanie and Nadia. Call Sumita and Brittany, they're on medical duty. We'll need L. M. and Ginnie Mae, too."

Madeline nodded at Jay as Athena ran off.

Jay watched the monitor of the cave complex as Sumita and Brittany loaded carts, presumably with medical supplies, into STACY. Ginnie Mae pushed a car repair cart. Athena paused at the control station.

"Put STACY right there." She pointed to a flat space near a freeway.

"Athena," Jay called through the intercom. "There's a 911 call in the city. Anaphylactic reaction. Ambulance can't get there; parents can't get the kid to the hospital."

"Show me the surrounding streets."

Jay complied, sending the images to Stephanie's station.

"Okay." Athena pointed, then called to Brittany. "Brittany, Stephanie's going to direct Arachne to where someone's having an anaphylactic reaction." She turned to Stephanie. "Then set it to where I pointed and I'll drive STACY through."

"Right." Stephanie said.

Jay gave Brittany the address to go to, and she went through with a backpack of medical supplies.

"By the way," Athena said to Stephanie, "I need to take your exoskeleton. I may have to move some cars." Without waiting for an answer, Athena adjusted her goggles and helmet and hurried away.

Stephanie turned. "It isn't sized for you."

Athena kept jogging, but called back, "I made some adjustments when you weren't looking."

"Go for it, then. Good luck." Stephanie faced her laptop again.

Soon after that, STACY rumbled through Arachne. Jay saw it emerge near a freeway.

Jay called STACY. "There's a pregnant woman stuck on the freeway, near you."

"Which car?" Athena asked.

Jay pinged the cell phone making the 911 call. "It's a blue Buick." He gave the license plate number.

Sumita and L. M. rushed out, threaded their way through the stalled cars, and carried the pregnant woman back to STACY, a bewildered-looking father-to-be following behind.

Jay's monitor showed Sumita making the pregnant woman comfortable on a cot, giving her reassurance and instructions while the mother-to-be grunted and groaned.

The father turned from Sumita to L. M., staring at the goggles and helmets. "Are you the National Guard?"

"No," said L. M., "we're the Emergency Choristers."

Jay heard Ginnie Mae laughing in the background.

Madeline, who had taken a seat beside Jay, sighed and shook her head.

"Okay, Jay," Athena called. "While we're waiting for the blessed event, give me the views of the freeway system. I want to see where the outlets are."

Jay showed her views of the traffic north, south, east, or west at Athena's command. Presumably Athena was seeing what she wanted on her own monitor screens; at intervals, she called out, "Save the GPS there as coordinate one," or two, three, four, etc.

While he was working, he heard Brittany call out to Stephanie and Nadia, "Okay, situation here under control. I've left enough medication to hold them in case of a biphasic reaction. Put a portal near me so I can get back to STACY."

Within seconds, Nadia called out, "Just walk straight north."

Jay had no monitor on the hall, but through the monitors on STACY, he saw Brittany arrive and assist Sumita in the delivery. After a healthy baby girl calmed down from her initial burst of crying, Sumita turned to the father. "Which hospital were you going to?"

When the father named the hospital, Jay found it.

"Sending Stephanie the coordinates," he called to Sumita's earpiece.

They told the father to lift up the mother, and once outside, Sumita, carrying the infant, led them through the portal. Seconds later, only Sumita came back.

Once Sumita was inside STACY again, Athena said, "Now, we're clearing traffic. Stephanie, send me to Jay's coordinate one."

"What's your plan?" Madeline called.

"If we get the cars moving at the end of the traffic lines, we can start to clear it."

"What about the ice and snow?"

"I have a heat ray and can warm the road as we go along. There's not much more than a coating; in these parts all it takes is a fraction of an inch to bring traffic to a halt. Temperature's risen to the lower 30s, which will make things easier."

"You're not going to fry anything, are you?"

"Hell, no, we only have to warm the pavement a degree or two. Once it's warm, it should hold the heat for a while until the front's passed."

"It's stopped drizzling for a while now," Ginnie Mae added.

To Jay, it seemed to be an impossible task. There had to be hundreds of miles of freeway, and thousands of cars on them. But slowly, Stacy moved from where traffic was light, and got the cars moving there, to where traffic was thickest. Sometimes Athena or Ginnie Mae had to get out and start a car. Other drivers, realizing what they were trying to do, pitched in to help with enthusiasm, moving other cars, leaving Athena or Ginnie Mae with the more difficult tasks of getting the long-haul trucks out of the way. Athena made full use of the exoskeleton to handle heavier vehicles. Occasionally STACY itself gave a machine an extra push.

Jay, Stephanie, and Nadia kept busy. Jay, between getting traffic views, picked up emergency calls where Sumita or Brittany were dispatched through portals to attend to medical emergencies, and then return.

Eventually, Athena called Stephanie and Nadia to bring STACY back to headquarters. Jay checked a clock and found they had been at it for five hours. It hardly had seemed five minutes.

Madeline put a hand on Jay's shoulder and stood. "Good work, Jay."

He looked up at her. "Thanks. You did your share of monitor work, too."

She smiled. "Well, the boss needs to do a little bit of everything in this sort of operation."

Jay turned to see Yolanda and Irene standing behind him.

"Don't worry. We held the fort while you were busy," Yolanda reassured him.

Jay gasped, realizing that he had totally forgotten the phone system.

Irene chuckled. "That's okay. We didn't have more orders than we could handle."

"Got a lot of orders for the mini-robots," Yolanda said with a smile. "This holiday season is going to be good for our bottom line."

"And Vivian got the uninterrupted design time she wanted," Irene added.

Madeline put an arm around Irene, and another around Yolanda. "Great job working backup, you two." She lowered her arms and walked toward the cave complex.

Jay, Irene, and Yolanda watched the cave monitors as Athena secured STACY. When its door opened and the ramp descended, their co-workers poured out, pulling off their masks, goggles, and helmets.

Brittany blew out a long breath. "Movie night!"

Within an hour, they all had assembled in Sumita and Brittany's living room. When everyone was settled on chairs or on the floor, they watched movie musicals on the large screen TV, singing along with some of the tunes. Between films, they switched to the cable news, which was full of videos taken of STACY appearing and disappearing, as well as hospital snapshots of Sumita or Brittany delivering patients and then winking out of sight.

"...and we have a name for the group now," the news anchor announced. "'The Emergency Choristers.'"

"L. M....," Madeline groaned.

"I kinda like it," Irene said.

Yolanda turned to Madeline. "Could have been a lot worse."

"Well, how was I to know they'd make so much of an offhand remark," L. M. protested.

Athena leaned back on her pillows and sipped the martini she had made for herself. "I can live with it."

"We can still pick another name, you know," Stephanie said. "Just tell people there was a mistake."

"I think 'Emergency Choristers' is okay," Ginnie Mae said.

"Yes, why not?" Daphne said.

"Should I embroider the name on the shirts?" Vivian asked cautiously. When everyone turned to her, she said, "What?"

Chapter 10

When the news showed a mine cave-in, and the experts the reporters interviewed said it would take a week or two just to drill to where the miners were, Madeline authorized the use of Arachne. At first, only L. M. and Sumita went through, but they came back quickly and asked for more help. Fortunately, all the miners had survived; unfortunately, some were trapped or injured and they needed extra hands and equipment to free the miners from rockslides, get them on stretchers, and move them through Arachne to hospitals. It wasn't long before the only employees at headquarters were Stephanie and Nadia in the cave complex plus Vivian, Yolanda, Irene, and Jay on the main floor. They all volunteered to help, but Madeline insisted that for safety's sake, it was best to deploy only those necessary to do the job, though they should be ready to go if additional help was needed.

Jay kept an eye on the monitor in the cave complex between routine business calls, and consciously looked up now and then, to see if anything else needed his attention. On one of those breaks, he noticed a truck with a long flatbed coming up the road. It had a long arm, reminding him of the "cherry pickers" that conveyed electrical workers up to repair high electrical lines...except all the electricity in the company complex and residence was either solar or geothermal; they were not connected to the grid.

He lifted his hands for a moment, thinking about what to do. The feeling that this meant big trouble was too strong to ignore. Irene had gone for coffee; he noticed her passing his desk a few minutes ago. Vivian was in her office, deep in her design work. Yolanda was on the phone with the Department of Commerce; he had connected the call earlier. He knew the call was important; they were expanding into international markets, and the Department of Commerce helped companies do that. Still....

Taking a breath, he typed into the digital dashboard that Athena had installed in every office after the first rescue mission. "Yolanda...trouble." Then he sat back, watching the truck approach. To his relief, the light on his dashboard showing the active call turned off. Outside, the truck stopped, and the long arm went up.

Yolanda approached Jay's desk. Looking outside, she said, "What's that truck doing...?"

BOOM!

The "cherry picker" at the end of the arm turned out to be a giant hammer. The building shook. Some dust on the roof from a recent sandstorm flew up, but no glass shattered, no walls crumbled.

Yolanda had reached Jay's desk. "Well, old Charles noticed that there was an emergency and guessed the building would be empty."

BOOM!

Vivian scrambled out of her office. "Stop that noise at once!"

Yolanda turned. "It isn't us, Vivian, and we'll find a way to stop it."

Irene rushed out of the stairway, carrying a covered cup of coffee. She stopped at Jay's desk. "Is that Charles again?"

BOOM!

"Shut up!" Vivian shouted.

Jay turned to Yolanda. "What do we do?"

"I think I can find something in your computer, if you'll let me have your chair for a minute."

Jay stood at once. "Be my guest."

She sat. "Let me see if I can activate the missiles."

Irene leaned over the console as Yolanda worked the keyboard. "How about I try the catapult?"

Yolanda kept her eye on the computer monitor, but said to Irene, "If you can do it safely."

BOOM!

"I'll do it!" Vivian shouted, and disappeared into the stairwell.

Yolanda sighed. "Irene, go after her and see she doesn't hurt herself."

Irene set her coffee on the ledge. "Right away." She ran after Vivian.

Jay put a hand on the back of the chair and leaned over to see the screen. "Missiles?"

Yolanda never took her eyes off the screen, which showed readouts that were unfamiliar to Jay. "Yes. Athena installed some early on, for defense, but Madeline decided our other defenses were better. Nadia did the programming. It may have been deleted, but I should be able to find it."

"I thought I'd found everything in the computer by now."

"Well, I've been trained to find things hidden in computers. You'd be surprised how embezzlers try to hide things from auditors...there it is."

BOOM!

Jay looked up. "How much of that can we take?"

"Oh, I'm sure it'll hold together, but the noise will get to us first. Good. Nadia made this pretty straightforward. Step one: line up target in the frame."

"The hammer?" Jay suggested.

"Well, it's not an explosive warhead, just a projectile, so I'd say try for a joint...there."

BOOM!

Jay noticed that even though the mechanism moved up and down, the frame moved with it.

"Step two: once the target is in the frame, click the unlock." She clicked it. "Step three: fire the missile by clicking the activate button." She glanced outside. "Need to wait for a pause."

BOOM!

Jay looked. The hammer rose, and the arm paused for a moment.

Yolanda clicked the mouse.

A long metal missile shot past the windows and hit the joint, bending it. Yolanda clicked again; another missile followed. Rocks fell from above on the arm and on the hammer. The result of the multiple impacts wrecked the mechanism. The operator seemed to try to get it to work; Jay heard the sounds of metal creaking from the outside monitors. The truck lumbered away.

Vivian hurried out of the stairwell, followed by Irene.

"We got it!" Vivian announced happily. She strode back to her office.

Irene walked to the console and picked up her coffee. After glancing to see Vivian was out of earshot, she said, "I did all the work."

Yolanda nodded. "I know, because you hit the target." She stood and with a gesture invited Jay to sit again.

He did. "Thanks. I'll tuck away the missile control system to where I can find it next time."

Yolanda nodded. "Can you get me the Department of Commerce again? I told them I would call back when I could."

"No problem!" Jay had them reconnected, and when he turned back to monitoring the team onsite, noticed with relief there was no one calling to ask why he had not been responding to requests.

Within a few hours, the news reported that the "Emergency Choristers" had freed and released all the miners. The company's team returned through Arachne. Soon they emerged from the cave complex, Madeline in the lead. They all looked exhausted and sooty.

"Let's just hit the showers," Madeline said wearily.

Vivian emerged from her office. "We were attacked!"

Everyone turned to her.

Yolanda stepped outside her office. "Charles again. Nothing we couldn't handle."

"Everything secure?" Madeline asked.

"We're fine," Yolanda assured her.

Madeline nodded. "We'll hear the story later. We're all going to grab something from the community freezer to heat and eat, then turn in early."

Silently, they filed into the passageway to the residence.

The next day, Jay came in at his usual time. The only others coming into the office were Stephanie, Nadia, Irene, Yolanda, and Vivian.

"It's just us today," Yolanda said. "The others had a real hard time. Madeline gave them all the day off to recover."

"I understand," Jay said.

At the end of the day, Irene approached his desk, carrying the flowers that Charles had sent them. They appeared to have been remarkably preserved. "Could you drive me to see my grandma? Madeline said I could give these flowers to her, and I need to hold onto the flower pot while in the car."

Jay rose from his chair. "Of course. Glad to help. Just tell me where."

When they were in the car, Irene gave directions, and they drove to a place labeled as an assisted living facility.

"You can come in if you want," Irene said. "Grandma always asks about my friends."

"Does she get many visitors?"

"No," Irene said matter-of-factly as they walked to the main entrance. "The rest of the family is either deployed or serving on bases in other states."

They signed in at the front desk. Jay noticed that Irene specified on the sign-in page that she had come to see "Edwina Williams."

Jay looked around as Irene led the way to her grandma. The place seemed to be in great condition. There were no bad smells, everything seemed to be clean. Units appeared to be modular, six or seven apartment-style units arranged around a central desk where staff gathered.

Edwina's apartment door, as all the apartment doors were in that module, was open. A large window had been set in the wall next to each door and all curtains were open so anyone could see inside any unit, at least at that moment. Irene walked in. Jay could see Edwina in a sort of small living room, sitting on a couch, reading a book. She had her feet on a long low table in front of her. A partition nearby sectioned off her bedroom, and beyond an open door, Jay could see a bathroom.

Irene set down the flowers. "Hi, Grandma, these are for you."

Edwina set down the book and stretched out her arms. "Hello, Irene, come see me." Irene leaned forward so Edwina could hug her; she gave her grandma a kiss as well. When she straightened up, she said, "This is Jay. He works in the same building I do."

Jay bowed slightly. "Pleased to meet you."

Edwina turned back to Irene. "He's nice, not like one of those strange men who were here."

"Strange men?" Jay asked.

"Yes, two of them. They came to see me. They said they knew Irene. They asked me about her and her job."

"What did you tell them, Grandma?"

"I told them to go away and leave me alone. I didn't like them."

"Well, if they come again, poke them in their stomachs and they'll go away."

"I will!" Edwina promised.

The two women began to talk about family matters, and Jay drifted into the center section. One of the staff members seemed intent on her computer screen, but when she paused and looked up, Jay asked, "Have there been any men visiting Ms. Williams lately?"

The staff member looked toward Edwina's apartment and then back to Jay. In a low voice, she said, "Mrs. Williams is in the early stages of dementia. She sometimes sees things that aren't there."

"Then there haven't been any men visiting her?"

"Except for you, no. She complained about a couple of men bothering her, but none of us saw anything unusual. We think she mistook a couple of orderlies or maintenance men for someone else."

"What about the monitors?"

"We had security check the recordings, but they said they didn't see anything out of the ordinary."

Jay nodded. He saw an older man, a resident presumably, park himself at a video game station in a recreational area of the module. He spotted Jay and invited Jay to join him with a gesture. Jay partnered with him on the game; the game ended just before Irene came for him.

On the drive back, he asked Irene, "Why did you say to your grandma to poke them in the stomach?"

"That's where the reset button is in the simulacrum. Terry says it activates a 'return to origin' command."

* * *

At the next staff meeting, Yolanda and Jay gave an account of the attack on the facility. Jay played the recording of the outside monitors, showing everything from the time the truck approached to the time it left.

"And thanks to Nadia for making the directions for the missiles so easy to follow," Yolanda concluded.

Nadia smiled. "You're welcome."

"Well, I see that I'll need to bring you up on the state of the defenses," Athena said.

"You can," Madeline said. "However, the building should be strong enough to resist anything short of a direct nuclear attack."

"I think we could survive even that," Athena said.

Madeline turned to Yolanda, Jay, Irene, and Vivian. "All you really need to do is to keep the doors locked."

"I can't work with all that racket going on!" Vivian complained.

"Just have Jay shut down the intercom to the outside," Madeline said. "It'll be quiet."

"There is the fact that the building shakes," Yolanda said.

"I see your point." Madeline turned to Athena. "Whenever you have a spare moment, go ahead and train them on whatever defense systems you think are best for the potential situations."

Things got back to normal quickly and Jay found himself handling calls and inquiries for the holiday season. One day, amidst all the communications, the caller ID on his screen said, "Charles Vance."

Jay stared at the screen for a second. It couldn't be, could it? Then he thought there was probably more than one "Charles Vance" in the world and perhaps this was a toy store owner in Detroit or somewhere.

He took the call. "Modern Surprises LLC, Jay Ecklund speaking. How may I help you?"

"This is Charles Vance. Please connect me with Madeline Chang."

Jay raised an eyebrow. That was him, all right. He recognized the voice from news reports. "One moment, please."

"This is an emergency," Charles said in a matter-of-fact tone.

"One moment," Jay repeated.

He flipped the intercom to Madeline's office. "Madeline, it's Charles on the phone. He says it's an emergency."

"Specifics?"

"That's all I got."

"Put him through. Monitor and record on your end."

"Will do." Jay flipped the appropriate controls.

"This is Madeline Chang. I understand there's an emergency?"

"Yes. My granddaughter and her geology class are in the California desert on a study trip. Their bus got hijacked on a deserted road when it broke down. The hijackers are herding the girls and their teachers to an unknown destination. My daughter gave my granddaughter a satellite phone and she's been sneaking communications when the hijackers haven't been looking. I've called the local authorities and they say it's going to take them a while to get there. You and I both know that those hijackers aren't going to patiently wait around for the authorities to intercept them."

"Why should I help you?"

"You're not helping me, you're helping my granddaughter and her classmates and their teachers. You won't let them get abused or sold off to who-knows-where, and you know that's what's going to happen. If they were being held for ransom, I and the other high-income parents and grandparents from the private girls' school would have been called by now."

"Have you tried calling them directly and making an offer?"

"Of course. No answer or an immediate hangup after the first syllable."

"Shall we make a deal, then? We do this rescue for you and you stop bothering us?"

"Would you trust me to make or keep a deal?"

"Now that you mention it, no." Madeline took a long breath. "Give us the satellite phone number and the location of the school. We'll take it from there."

"Although I know it doesn't mean much, thank you."

"You're right; it doesn't mean much at all. Mr. Ecklund is coming on the line; give the information to him."

Jay took the cue, got the information from Charles, and unceremoniously hung up. By that time, Madeline was at his desk.

"Get a satellite view of the location, Jay."

While Jay was working, Madeline got on the intercom to call everyone over to his desk. When they arrived, she quickly explained the situation.

"You didn't cut a deal?" Athena said.

"Ha!" Yolanda said. "As if he would keep one."

L. M. spoke with a toothpick in her mouth. "Bad guys always have our number. They know the good guys will always come through on principle."

"Too bad we can't walk away from this," Athena said.

"We can't," L. M. agreed, "otherwise we'd be the bad guys."

Terry, meanwhile, leaned over Jay and examined the screen intently. It showed a desert setting. A loose group of teenage girls, a couple of young women, and an older woman in a bus driver's uniform walked in the midst of armed men not too much older than the girls. Two open-top gray jeeps drove slowly alongside.

Terry raised her head. "Human traffickers. The private detectives I hired investigated them, thinking that maybe they had made off with my family. They'll sell them off to the highest bidder, or keep some of them for themselves."

"Not if we have anything to say about it," Daphne said.

Terry turned to Madeline. "I think it's time to bring out Nightmare."

Madeline nodded. "I agree."

"Can I bring my gun?" Terry asked.

"I don't want you to kill them, if it can be avoided."

"I won't," Terry promised.

"I'm coming, too." L. M. smiled. "Kick some butt!"

"You're not going to fire a high energy bolt at them?" Athena said.

"Hell, no, I'm taking the projectile gun. It'll just knock them over like bowling pins."

"Lose the toothpick," Madeline said.

In an easy motion, L. M. pinched the toothpick and expertly flipped it into a nearby trash bin.

Jay put the satellite feed on the wide screen, so that everyone could see it. First, Stephanie and Nadia put L. M. behind the advancing group. Seemingly confident in their isolation, none of the armed guards ever looked back. L. M. positioned herself behind a convenient boulder. She settled the projectile gun on top, took careful aim, and hit the rear guard in the back with what appeared to Jay to be a small plastic sphere roughly the size of a baseball. The guard went down.

At the same time, the robot appeared in front of the group, letting out a bloodcurdling roar that made Jay want to hide under his desk. The robot grabbed the jeeps, one in each paw; the occupants jumped out and Nightmare tossed the vehicles aside. Some of the girls screamed; all the captives ran toward L. M. Most of the guards ran toward the shelter of the overturned jeeps, though some took aim at the robot and fired. Jay was afraid that the bullets would ricochet and hurt someone, but Nightmare's hide seemed to absorb or trap the bullets. A couple of guards made a move to try to corral the girls again, but L. M. took them out. Then, like a traffic officer, L. M. stood and motioned the fleeing girls and women in a certain direction. Whether they recognized L. M. as one of the "Emergency Choristers" because of her goggles and helmet, or whether they just trusted someone who was not one of the hijackers, they obeyed, and disappeared.

Jay's destination satellite screen showed the group appearing in the school's parking lot.

Meanwhile, Nightmare's claws reached down and snatched guns from the hands of the hijackers, squashing the weapons and tossing them aside. Some of the hijackers ran; others tried to beat the robot with their hands, hurting themselves.

Once all the girls were gone, and the hijackers either runnng away or incapacitated, Nightmare stopped. A door opened in one of Nightmare's shins. Terry climbed out and motioned to L. M., who ran toward her. One of the hijackers lying on the ground made a move to grab one of the smashed long guns, presumably to use it as a club against L. M.; Terry drew her gun lightning-fast and shot the weapon, making it flip on the sand away from the hijacker. L. M. also saw the motion and almost simultaneously used the projectile gun. The ammo sphere hit the man in the stomach.

After that, the remaining hijackers made no threatening moves as Terry and L. M. climbed into Nightmare. Soon, Nightmare turned around, walked a couple of steps, and disappeared.

When the cave complex monitor showed Nightmare had come home, Madeline turned to the others around Jay's desk. "I assume Charles can take it from here."

Within the hour, Sam had made another delivery of flowers with a card that simply said THANK YOU. The cable news showed cell phone pictures of Nightmare and of L. M. directing traffic. A reporter on the scene in California got a statement from the local authorities that they had picked up the hijackers, who had an amazing story about a green monster that came out of nowhere and disappeared again.

Chapter II

Everyone left the residence for Thanksgiving except Jay and Terry. L. M. had invited them to join the Yeagers, but they declined. Instead, they got together in Terry's apartment and ate a warmed-up pre-cooked turkey loaf.

"Mmmm, not bad," Jay said as he tasted the main course.

"I've definitely had worse," Terry agreed. "Plus we have ice cream imported from the Yeagers for dessert."

Jay nodded. "That's a plus. I really didn't feel comfortable imposing on their Thanksgiving, despite the invitation."

"Me, neither," Terry said. "I've felt like the fifth wheel on others' Thanksgiving celebrations."

"I know the feeling, too."

"Madeline told me about your family disowning you...I hope that was all right."

"Of course. That's not a secret."

"You must have seen the headline I showed Charles's simulacrum."

He nodded. "That must have been tough. I can't imagine what you must have gone through."

She sighed. "There was a family reunion when I was in college between my sophomore and junior years; we rented a lodge in the woods. I left for a day to go to a concert nearby, and when I drove back, they were gone. Cars gone, suitcases gone. No sign of any struggle; the lodge was clean, beds made, rugs vacuumed, dishes washed and put away. No answer on any phone. No one ever returned home. No evidence of credit card use. Police, detectives I hired, no one ever found a thing."

"No motive, either?"

Terry shook her head. "None the detectives or I could ever determine."

"No enemies, no long-standing grudges from third parties?"

"None that I knew of. We checked, of course...asked neighbors, current and old. Nothing turned up."

"I am sorry."

Terry nodded. "I consider everyone here to be my family now."

"So do I."

After dinner, they watched a couple of Westerns together. Occasionally Jay glanced to Terry's bookshelf, where Widget, in her cage, munched on her hamster meal. When the second movie ended, Jay stood. "Since neither of us has any reason to hit the sales tomorrow, how about joining me at the Dry Cactus bar for brunch? They have a real nice after-Thanksgiving spread."

Terry nodded. "Sounds like a plan."

The next day, they drove in Jay's car and were some of the first to take advantage of the buffet. Jay ordered his weekly beer; Terry ordered one, as well.

Don stopped at their table. "Well, hello, haven't seen you in a while, Jay."

Jay motioned to Terry. "Terry, this is Don, my former boss. Don, Terry's one of my co-workers."

They nodded at each other. "Pleased to meet you," Don said. "Could I sit and visit for a minute?"

"Be my guest," Jay said.

Don took a chair and sat at their table. "I wanted to tell you, Jay, that I found an angel investor and started my own business. I'm hiring, and you're welcome to join me if you want." He turned to Terry before Jay could answer. "I'm sure I could find a place for you, too."

Terry smiled. "Thanks for the offer, but no."

Jay shook his head. "I'm happy for you, Don, but I'm settled where I am."

Don nodded. "Okay, but if you ever change your minds, the offer's open." He stood, put the chair back, and waved a farewell.

The brunch, as usual, was delicious. Terry said she would make a note and maybe come again next year. On their drive back, they ran into a police blockade. An officer directed them around a barrier of sawhorses.

"Wonder what's going on there?" Terry asked.

"Not sure," Jay said.

Terry reached for the radio controls. "Mind if I try the radio?"

"Go ahead. News is at 86.3 AM."

The station broadcasted breaking news. By the time they reached the residence, they heard that the antiquities vault at the museum had accidentally closed, trapping a tour group and tour guide inside. The commentator stated that the museum officials insisted that the vault had been designed not to close unintentionally. They added that the backups installed to open it in case of an unforeseen lockdown had failed. They were in contact with the group through a phone in the vault, and all were well for the moment, with enough air for several hours, at least, but one of the visitors was a diabetic who would need his regular insulin injection soon. The authorities had brought experts to try to open the vault, so far without success.

When Jay parked the car underneath the residence, he leaned over to Terry. "I'm going to my desk in headquarters and see if I can tap into the museum's monitors."

Terry nodded. "I'll come with you."

They sat at Jay's desk while he tuned into the monitors. There was a camera in the vault, showing about twenty people among the display stands, some milling around, some sitting on the floor surrounding a man covered with a jacket. One woman wearing a museum name tag seemed to be talking on a wall phone.

Terry put a finger on the screen. "That tourist is a simulacrum. So's that one. That one, too. The rest are humans."

"This is Charles, baiting us," Jay said.

Terry nodded. "He's hoping that we'll take the tourists through Arachne—then the simulacrums would break away from us and go into the cave complex."

Jay turned to Terry. "How would they know that much?"

"Not the specifics, no. But he knows there's a way to get into Arachne and from Arachne, to get to here. I'd bet after his granddaughter was rescued, Charles invited her over for tea for a long conversation with Grandpa to tell him all about her experience."

"She would have seen the portals within Arachne."

Terry nodded.

"So he's hoping the simulacrums will come in and steal Arachne," Jay said.

"Pretty hard to do, given its size and mass. They'd probably try to find the plans."

"...Or take pictures, readings, whatever."

"That probably wouldn't work," Terry said. "The shell is made of special material Athena came up with that would block any kind of scan."

Jay turned back to the screen. "What do we do then? Nothing? I suppose the safecracking experts could get in eventually, couldn't they?"

Terry sighed. "Gosh, I don't know. But I wouldn't want to try to use Arachne to rescue them without Madeline knowing."

"How about asking L. M.? She invited us to the Yeagers, after all. She shouldn't mind us calling."

"Sure. That'll work."

Jay dialed up L. M. from the desk. She answered right away. "What's up, Jay? Why are you calling from the company phone?"

"We have a situation." He explained quickly.

"Let me take a look at it before you call Madeline. Can you dial up the estate?"

"I can," Terry called.

"Good. Meet you there."

In the cave complex, Terry booted up Stephanie's laptop and dialed the Yeager estate. Jay watched closely, noticing the steps she took. Nadia had apparently standardized the procedure; the instructions on the screen seemed clear and straightforward.

When L. M. came through, toothpick in mouth, and walked around the barrier, Jay said, "Sorry to interrupt your Thanksgiving weekend."

L. M. waved the remark away. "Just having a family jam session. Besides, if Charles is up to something, I want to know about it."

Jay commandeered Nadia's laptop and showed L. M. the scene inside the vault. L. M. examined the view closely. The toothpick went up and down as she studied the screens. Eventually, she straightened and twirled the toothpick thoughtfully.

"Hm. Now Charles wouldn't want a death on his hands. He would have planned a way out, just in case."

"Sure he has," Jay said. "Us."

L. M. shook her head. "But what if we didn't respond? I'll bet he has an expert who can open the vault that he'll bring up at the last minute if we don't act, probably the same agent who found a way to 'accidentally' close the vault."

"So we do nothing and let Charles's expert save the day?" Jay said.

L. M. sighed. "Not necessarily. Charles's agent could fail to open it, too, or something else could go wrong in the meantime." She tapped the toothpick thoughtfully. "Besides, if we take Charles's bait, we may be able to send the message not to mess with us. Let me call Madeline." She took out her cell phone, then paused. "Come to think of it, better text her. She's probably out in some crowded mall with the nephews."

Jay leaned over and saw L. M. text, "Got situation. Use company assets?"

Moments later, the answer came: "Just saw it on the news. Go ahead. Use discretion. Watch for imposters."

L. M. texted: "Will do." She put the cell phone back in her pocket.

"What's the plan?" Jay said.

L. M. took over Stephanie's laptop. "Terry and I will get the tourists out. We'll line them up single file with the simulacrums last. I'll place the exit portal in the park next to the museum."

"What if a simulacrum breaks away and comes here?" Jay asked.

"I designed the panic robot just for this situation," Terry said. "It's supposed to scare humans, but it will also confuse the simulacrums and their handlers."

"Panic robot?" Jay asked.

"Remember your first day here?" Terry said.

Jay opened his mouth wide. "Oh, yeah, *that* robot!"

L. M. motioned to the barrier between them and Arachne. "We'll put the robot right in front of Arachne."

"I'll set a motion sensor," Terry said. "If anything emerges from Arachne, the robot will activate."

"What if it's you?" Jay said.

L. M. tilted her head toward him. "Jay, it's harmless, remember? Terry and I won't be afraid of it."

"...But it will disorient the simulacrums," Terry said.

"Sounds good," Jay said.

Terry and L. M. retrieved the robot. Jay walked along as they positioned it. As Terry made adjustments, Jay looked toward the barrier and found "Home Sweet Home" painted on it.

L. M. turned toward it. "Daphne complained that it was hard getting her bearings just seeing a gray wall, so Irene got some stencils and paint and lettered it."

"Doesn't that mean that anyone within Arachne will see it?" Jay asked.

Terry straightened up. "Yes, if they're close enough and looking in the right place."

"Better than seeing the entire cave complex," L. M. said. She and Terry went to the curtained booths to get their uniforms, masks, and goggles on. When they emerged, L. M. went to Stephanie's laptop and activated Arachne.

"Just leave it there," she said to Jay. "We'll adjust it when we come back. Put a satellite on the museum park and monitor the vault in case there's trouble."

"Though I'm not anticipating any," Terry said.

L. M. tossed her toothpick into a nearby wastebasket. "You never know."

Through the monitor, Jay watched as L. M. and Terry emerged in the vault and lined up the tourists. Jay counted twenty-three, including the museum tour guide with the name badge. Then, one by one, they began to emerge in the park. Jay counted twenty, and then...nothing. He checked the vault monitor. No one there. The simulacrums must be giving them trouble, he thought.

He walked to the barrier, next to the panic robot. Suddenly, L. M. and a simulacrum appeared, grappling. The simulacrum had one hand at the back of L. M.'s neck. Its other hand squeezed her upper arm. Immediately, the panic robot activated, making Jay jump before he remembered it was harmless. When he turned his attention back to L. M., she had an arm around the simulacrum. The simulacrum calmly allowed L. M. to guide it into Arachne again.

Jay rushed to Nadia's laptop. The monitor on the park showed Terry escorting two simulacrums out; moments later, L. M. emerged, still guiding the last simulacrum. While the human tourists milled around, Terry and L. M. pushed the simulacrums in the stomach. They ambled away. L. M. and Terry took a couple of steps and disappeared.

Moments later, L. M. rushed out, ignoring the panic robot's racket. The instant she reached Stephanie's laptop, she watched to make sure Terry had come through and put Arachne on standby. Terry shut off the panic robot.

L. M. turned to Jay. "Had to make sure that no one tried to follow us back."

Jay shook his head and motioned to the monitor screen. "I haven't seen anyone even make the attempt."

"Good," L. M. said. "Now why don't you and Terry come back to the estate with me? Terry can ride the horses, and I'm sure Cousin Andy would give you a tour of the complex, Jay. He's in charge of the communications systems, and would just love to have someone he can talk shop to."

Terry shook her head. "Thanks, but I told the Santanas that I'd be riding my horse starting tomorrow."

L. M. nodded and turned to Jay. "How about you?"

Jay waved at Arachne. "Not sure how it would affect my brain."

L. M. looked at Arachne, and then back to Jay. "Did you want to wait until Sumita comes back and checks you out before trying it?"

Jay considered. He could go, or he could face a long, lonely weekend with Terry out riding. He squared his shoulders. "Oh, what the hell, I'll try it. Just give me a few minutes to go to the residence and pack an overnight bag."

When he returned, Terry dialed the Yeager estate. Jay held the handle of his overnight bag in one hand.

L. M. took his free arm. "We'll walk slowly, and if you're feeling as if you're having trouble, we can come back."

Jay nodded. He took a deep breath before they stepped into Arachne. Once in, he heard singing. He stopped. Looking up, it seemed as if Arachne had a vaulted ceiling. Turning straight ahead, he could see the Yeager estate.

"Are you okay, Jay?" L. M. asked.

"Yes, I hear singing."

L. M. tilted her head. "I hear her usual music, that is, tonal sounds, but I haven't heard any singing for a while. Are there any words?"

"No. It...it reminds me of when I was in Europe. I sat in a cathedral once while a women's chorus was practicing. No words, just aah–aah–aah–aah–aah."

"How's your head?"

"Oh, it's fine." He smiled, realizing that he really felt fine.

"Good. Let's go out before Terry thinks something went wrong."

They stepped out onto the Yeager estate. L. M. let go of his arm. Jay turned. He could not see anything that would define a portal.

"Hear any singing now?"

He turned to her. "No, do you?"

"No, the music stops when I step out. Just wondering. How do you feel?"

He put his free hand to his chest. "Energized. As if I'd had a long, restful sleep."

She smiled. "That's Arachne for you."

The Monday after Thanksgiving, Madeline called a staff meeting. "Jean's taken an extra few days off, to celebrate the start of Hanukkah, but we can fill her in when she gets back. Jay and Terry, tell everyone what happened here over the weekend."

After they had told their story, Athena shook her head. "I never thought I'd miss those simulacrums, but I wouldn't mind having some now, at least to create some mischief with the ones Charles has."

Stephanie turned to Terry. "Can you design something similar? Something that wouldn't trespass on the rights Charles bought? Ginnie Mae, Athena, and I would be happy to help you."

Terry took a breath and shook her head. "It took me months just to come up with the basic design...."

Yolanda tapped her pen on the desk. "I'm glad this subject came up, because I've been thinking we ought to go and buy some."

"Buy from Charles? He'd never let us," L. M. said.

"Not Charles; the factory on the east coast," Yolanda said.

"Can we do that?" Nadia asked.

"Surely Charles told them not to sell them to anybody," Daphne said.

"Not directly, no," Yolanda said. "But I've seen the contract he made with the factory; it had to be filed publicly with the local government, and was therefore accessible to me. There's a sublicensure agreement that allows the main factory to contract with other factories to make them; and further clauses stating the factory can retain simulacrums for quality control tests and company use."

"Among other cracks and crevices in the wording that we can take advantage of," Madeline added.

"Possibly we can make a deal under the table," Athena said, "though you didn't hear me say that."

"Sounds fine to me." L. M. reached behind her to scratch between her shoulder blades.

Daphne, sitting next to her, looked over. "What's that?"

L. M. put her hand down. "Just an itch."

Daphne stood. "No, I saw something. Sumita, take a look." She pulled back the collar of L. M.'s shirt as Sumita walked over. "What do you make of that?"

Sumita looked from L. M. to Daphne. "I'd need to get a magnifier to be sure."

"Oh, I'm sure," Daphne bent down to look L. M. in the face. "You've been chemically tagged."

"What?" said several voices at once.

Jay gestured at L. M. "When the simulacrum was grappling with L. M., it had a hand on the back of her neck. Could it have been implanting something?"

Athena stood and waved at L. M. "Come on, I need to scan you."

"Like the scanner at the entrance?" Jay asked.

"I have a booth in the cave complex, does the same thing." Athena waved at L. M. again. "Come on."

They all followed Athena and L. M. to a device that resembled an airport scanner that one walked through. "Just stand under it," Athena said.

Jay stood next to Athena as she worked the control panel and looked over the monitor readout. "Let's see, no electronics, so L. M. hasn't been 'chipped.'"

"You mean like a pet?" Ginnie Mae asked.

"Exactly what I mean," Athena said, "but no evidence of that. Still, I'm reading strong but harmless emissions on the EM spectrum. With the right equipment, I could track you and get a GPS history of your movements."

Daphne nodded. "Chemical tag, just as I said."

"Can you get it off me?" L. M. said.

"I can excise a layer of skin," Sumita said.

"No need. I have solvents," Daphne said.

"Then you get the solvents; I have ointments that will help it heal. I'll take L. M. and we'll meet at my office." Sumita pointedly turned to the others. "You can stay here and wait."

"We'll meet you in the staff room," Madeline said. When they left, she turned to Athena. "Scan Terry and Jay, just to be sure."

To Jay's great relief, the scans on Terry and him showed nothing.

"What if there had been something?" Jay asked Athena after he had been scanned.

Athena indicated the controls. "This setting wipes any memory cards clean, and this one shuts off any transmitters."

Jay nodded.

They walked back to the staff room. Soon Sumita, Daphne, and L. M. joined them. Jay could see the end of a gauze pad on L. M.'s neck.

Madeline placed her folded hands on the table. "All right, what could Charles find out from that tracking?"

"He already knows where we are; that won't do him any good," Vivian said.

"He's trying to measure the location of Arachne's apertures," Stephanie said, "where they begin, where they end, how wide they are, and so forth."

"But no signals can come out from within Arachne," Nadia said.

"That's right," Stephanie said, "but when L. M. stepped out of Arachne and stepped back in, Charles knew exactly where the aperture was."

"How would knowing where the portal was at the museum park help him?" Terry said.

"It would give him a general...," Stephanie began.

Jay gasped. "The Yeager estate! We went back and forth from the Yeager estate! He knows where our alternate site is and where we place the portals there."

Madeline rubbed an eyebrow and turned to L. M. "Notify your family. They may be getting visitors."

L. M. let out a breath. "Will do. Though they're always on the alert for intruders."

"We sure blew it, didn't we?" Vivian said.

"I hate to burst anyone's bubble," Brittany said, "but it's inevitable that we're going to make mistakes. None of us is perfect."

Irene leaned forward. "My father always said that mistakes are where you learn to do better next time."

"If there's any blame, assign it to me," Madeline said. "I authorized the operation."

"I admit being a little hot under the collar right now," Athena said, "but it could have happened to anyone, including me. Charles was going to peck at us until he had an opening."

"So, what do we do now?" Ginnie Mae asked.

"Let me go back to what we were discussing earlier," Yolanda said. "I say, let's see if we can buy a simulacrum."

"Or two," Athena said.

Chapter 12

Although most physical stores had ordered and received their holiday items well before Thanksgiving, the company's web division was expected to remain busy right up until December 24. While contractors handled most of the work, company headquarters still had a large number of inquiries to handle and would stay open at least until the 20th. Jay kept up with the traffic.

A sudden, fierce storm came up in a remote area. Jay picked up a call that a couple of campers were in danger of being washed away, and too far from the nearest emergency responders to rescue. Madeline dispatched L. M. and Stephanie, who quickly got the campers to safety.

Jay, as usual, watched the monitors when they came back.

"Any problems?" Madeline asked.

L. M. tore off her helmet, goggles, and mask. "None."

Stephanie turned to Madeline. "I noticed something. There was a hurricane-force wind out there; the rain was nearly horizontal."

L. M. took a box from her pocket and drew out a toothpick. "Yeah, that's why the first thing we did was anchor a cable to a rock so we wouldn't be blown away."

"But when we went back into Arachne, the wind and rain didn't follow us. It was completely dry, and calm."

L. M. bit on her toothpick. "That's how we want it, don't we?"

Nadia leaned over from the control station. "I wonder if we could make an underwater rescue."

Madeline tapped her chin thoughtfully. "Now, that's an idea."

"If we can be sure the water won't rush into Arachne and flood the cave complex here...," Stephanie said.

"Maybe you can design a test where you put the aperture partway underwater, say about six inches, and have someone wade toward it," Madeline said. "That should tell us something, shouldn't it?"

"Yes, we could try that," Stephanie said.

"Well, get together with everyone who has offices in the cave complex first to make sure that everything's off the floor in case we get flooded," Madeline said. "Then you can try it."

Along with Madeline and Stephanie, Jay thought such a test would be a great idea, and was surprised when the suggestion met with resistance. Most of the women in the cave complex did not want to spend the time and energy to take precautions for a flood, especially during this busy season when they also had to take so many product inquiries. A compromise was reached in which everyone promised to pitch in after the holiday season was over.

However, Fate seemed to have other plans. Jay picked up a phone call from a tourist ship sinking in the Mediterranean. When it was clear that no ship could come to the rescue in time, Madeline got on the intercom and told everyone to brace for water. Jay heard no objections to the operation.

Daphne, who was a Coast Guard veteran, boarded the ship with L. M. They appeared on the bridge of the vessel. Quickly, Daphne told Stephanie exactly where to place the portal and told her they were going to steer into it. Jay provided the coordinates of the nearest clear beach with a long empty dock. Moments later, the satellite monitor on the Mediterranean showed the ship disappear...and the satellite monitor on the beach showed the ship appearing next to the dock and leaning into it.

Jay quickly checked the cave complex monitor. The cave had remained completely dry. Less than a minute later, Daphne and L. M. walked in.

Daphne pulled off her helmet and goggles. "The boat slid right though Arachne, smooth as silk, and not a drop of water followed us from either end."

"How does it know how to do that?" Ginnie Mae asked. She had remained near the control station with Athena throughout the operation, watching the monitors.

Stephanie held up her hands and shrugged.

"Well, you ought to know, you designed it," Athena said.

L. M. chuckled. "Arachne has grown beyond all of us."

Madeline looked Stephanie steadily in the eye. "You know what this means, don't you? We can set a portal in space."

Stephanie's face broke into a wide grin.

Jay was beginning to wonder if Fate, indeed, had been listening in on their conversations, because not long afterwards, the news reported that a terrorist with a barrel bomb had invaded a coffee shop in Amsterdam. More precisely, he had driven a truck carrying the bomb straight through the front plate glass window, had somehow rolled the barrel from the truck to the coffee shop floor, and currently was threatening to detonate it. Because the terrorist claimed that the bomb contained sarin gas canisters, the authorities had ordered a citywide evacuation. The streets leading away from the city were clogged with traffic.

Madeline studied the satellite view at Jay's desk and sighed. She turned to the others who had crowded around. "It's too bad that we can't sweep the portal from one side of the bomb to the other, pick it up, and deposit it into space."

Jay looked up. "Couldn't you?"

Madeline shook her head. "Arachne doesn't work that way. Stephanie has tried. We have to somehow physically pick up the bomb and shove it through Arachne."

"Hell, any wheelie cart can do that," L. M. said, looking over their shoulders. "Our problem is the terrorist in the way."

Athena waved at the screen. "I don't see a dead man switch or a plunger in his hand. There's a timer on the barrel, counting down, and a button next to it, which I presume can set it off independently of the timer."

"Meaning that if he's not able to hit the button, the timer will still detonate it," L. M. said.

"Why not shoot him and then try to disassemble the timer?" Ginnie Mae asked.

L. M. shook her head. "Not enough time."

Athena pointed to the screen. "That kind of timer will set off the bomb anyway if tampered with."

Madeline straightened up and took a breath. "It seems that we somehow have to get past the terrorist, put the bomb on a cart, and get it into Arachne. And fast."

L. M. turned to Madeline, bit on her toothpick, and grinned. "Piece of cake. Want to flip to see who gets the terrorist?"

As Madeline and L. M. were suiting up, Stephanie called Jay on the intercom. "Jay, can you get me a location in space that's fairly empty?"

"On it," Jay said.

Most of the others had gone into the cave complex, but Vivian, Yolanda, and Irene still huddled around his desk. "Can you put it in orbit above us?" Irene said. "I'd like to see it blow up."

Jay nodded. Since Irene had mentioned it, he realized he could do just that. In fact anywhere 50 to 100 miles farther from the low Earth orbit that most satellites occupied would do.

After giving Stephanie the coordinates, they watched quietly as Madeline and L. M.–without the toothpick—walked into Arachne. Madeline had a coil of rope and a heavy net slung over an arm. L. M. pushed a wheelie cart.

Jay turned his attention to the satellite monitor overlooking the Amsterdam coffee shop. Police cruisers had surrounded it and someone with a horn spoke to the terrorist. When Madeline and L. M. did not appear on the screen right away, he zoomed in a bit. He still did not see them.

"They'll watch from inside Arachne until the terrorist is facing toward the street and stepping away from the bomb for a moment." When Jay turned to Yolanda, she added, "Family in the army, remember? Counter-terrorism unit."

Fortunately, the terrorist seemed very eager to shout at the authorities surrounding him. He took two steps in their direction. Immediately, Madeline and L. M. appeared behind him. Madeline threw the net over his head, shoulders, and upper arms. She tied it close to his body with the rope, even as he struggled in vain. Meanwhile, L. M. got the wheelie cart next to the bomb. She and Madeline got the barrel onto the cart's ledge and quickly disappeared back into Arachne. Within seconds, they emerged, cartless, into the cave complex.

"Mission accomplished," Madeline breathed. "We pushed the cart right into the void."

"Portals closed," Stephanie said.

Irene pointed outside. "Let's see it blow up."

They rushed outdoors and looked up. Nothing caught their attention.

"There were some seconds left," Yolanda remarked.

Within a minute, they were joined by their coworkers from the cave complex.

Stephanie pointed. "There it is."

Even in the sunlit afternoon, they clearly saw a light brighten, spread, and dim. When they went back inside, the cable news showed the Amsterdam authorities leading the terrorist, net still tied around him, away.

At a staff meeting in mid-December, Vivian unveiled her project for next year: dolls, or more precisely, action figures for girls, complete with wardrobe and accessories so that the doll could be an astronaut, police officer, firefighter, and so forth.

After Vivian received admiration all around, Yolanda took the floor. "No progress in getting a simulacrum. I tried getting the factory's attention directly, and then tried through our toy divisions. It seems that Charles has alerted them of the identities of all our subsidiaries so that we're blocked at every turn."

"How about making one up?" Athena asked.

Yolanda shook her head. "Our names are known to him, and the identity of any DBA must be made public by law."

"I could help." When everyone turned to her, Terry elaborated. "My uncle had a business making and selling souvenir pins. After he disappeared with the rest of the family, there was still a large inventory that I've been selling from his website. It's only a few hundred dollars a month, but the business is still active and in his name, though I inherited it when I finally got his death certificate."

"Are you still filing schedule Cs?" Yolanda asked.

Terry nodded. "Every year."

"Take credit card orders?" Yolanda asked.

"Oh, yes," Terry said.

Yolanda turned to Madeline. "Then the business has an active credit rating."

Madeline smiled and placed her folded hands on the table, leaning toward Terry. "How would you like to become a wholly-owned subsidiary of Modern Surprises LLC?"

* * *

In contrast to Thanksgiving, Jay found the residence over the winter holidays less empty. Although Daphne had gone for her own winter celebration, he, Terry, Athena, Nadia, Jean, Sumita, and Brittany remained. He and Terry each had a Christmas tree in their respective apartments; Athena had put up a solstice tree in hers. They all gathered for a solstice celebration at Athena's on the 21st. Terry and Jay got together and threw a party at Terry's apartment on Christmas Eve; everyone there came to that one, too.

Madeline had given everyone a generous holiday bonus. In addition, they had a company gift exchange—a generic gift to be opened whenever the recipient felt like it. Terry had drawn Jay's name, and as a result, on Christmas Day, Jay had a wrapped package under his tree to open, as well as a filled stocking Terry had given him to hang up the day before. He opened the box and found a Stetson. Immediately, he put the hat on and stood in front of a mirror, admiring the effect. He left it on as he went to the computer and emailed a thank you note to Terry. In his inbox, he saw a thank you from Ginnie Mae for the baseball jersey he had given her. He also saw an invitation from Nadia to everyone at the residence to play mini-golf that afternoon. Jay wore his hat to the tournament and found Terry wearing a similar hat.

Company headquarters had closed from the 20th through New Year's. Jay woke on the 26th rubbing his chin and declaring to himself that this was a "no-shave" day. After breakfast, he checked his email, and found a note from Athena: If you're as bored as I am, meet me in the back for a game of croquet.

When Jay arrived, he saw everyone else at the residence there.

"What, no one going to the post-holiday sales?" Brittany asked with a smile.

"And get crushed by the crowds? No, thanks," Nadia said.

As Jay leaned on his mallet, watching the others, waiting for his turn, the smartphone in his pocket buzzed. He picked it up and saw it was from L. M. He put it on speaker. "Merry Christmas," he said.

"We had one yesterday, yes," L. M. said. "Today's a nightmare. We heard heavy trucks rumbling by in the morning—no surprise there, that happens just about every day. Then, just when Uncle Zach was about to open the barn doors and let the livestock out for the day, here come the simulacrums. The electric fences didn't stop 'em. Zach locked the barn and ran back to the main building before the simulacrums caught up with him."

Athena walked over to Jay and spoke into the phone. "So? They're harmless. Just let them wander around until their power packs run out of charge."

"There are hundreds of them," L. M. said. "Aunt Thelma and Uncle Ned went to the roof of the main building, thinking about picking them off, but there are just too many of them. It seems more are coming in by the minute."

"You know that Charles just wants us to open up Arachne so he can come in here," Athena said. "With hundreds running around, chances are some simulacrum will walk through a portal no matter where we put it."

"There's the panic robot," Jay said. "That deterred them before."

Athena turned to Jay. "What if there's a human agent among the simulacrums? With hundreds out there, it would be like trying to spot a needle in a haystack."

Terry walked up to Jay. "How about generating an EMP? That will stop them."

"Can't do it," L. M. said. "We're an emergency shelter for the county because they rely on us to have power no matter what."

Jay spoke into the phone. "What does Madeline say?"

"Hasn't responded to my text, yet."

"I still don't see why you can't just let them wander around," Athena said.

L. M. sighed. "There are a dozen reasons. We have animals to graze, businesses to run, a public New Year's celebration to start setting up...."

Terry's phone beeped. She took it out of her pocket. "It's Madeline," she said, and answered it. "Hi, Madeline, we're on the phone with L. M."

"Good. Her line was busy. Look, we all know this is a trap, but the Yeagers have been more than generous with us and we have to help them. Using STACY and Nightmare together, you ought to be able to clean up the simulacrums in good time. I'll pay you double salary for your effort, of course."

Athena leaned over. "I don't care about the money, I care about the possible security breach."

"Set up the panic robot and leave at least one person in the cave complex to guard it. Before you go to the Yeager estate, bring me in. I'll give more instructions when I get there."

"Should we bring in the others?" Terry asked.

"No...on second thought, call Yolanda and see if she wants in. Daphne's local; call her, too. If either decline, let them stay where they are."

Jay called Daphne and Yolanda from the croquet court; both said they wanted to come in. Once in the cave complex, Nadia took charge of Arachne and brought in Madeline, Yolanda, and L. M. They all got suited up; even Jay went into his designated booth for the first time and put on the uniform shirt, pants, and boots, though he left off the mask, goggles, and helmet.

Jay left the booth and took over Stephanie's laptop. He got a satellite view of the Yeager estate; Nadia reached over and input some commands. After consulting the screen, she looked up. "The computer counted 1452 simulacrums."

Madeline nodded and turned to the others. "Here's the plan: Terry takes Nightmare, Athena takes STACY."

"And the rest of us?" Brittany asked.

"We have an entire motor pool at the estate," L. M. said. "We have tractors, combines, harvesters...."

"Too bad you don't have an MRAP," Sumita said with a smile. "I drove one when I was in the service."

"Got one of those, too," L. M. said matter-of-factly.

Sumita raised an eyebrow.

"The rest of us go there and take whatever we can drive," Madeline said.

"I'm staying inside Arachne," Daphne said. "No one's getting past me."

"That's a good idea," Madeline said. "The panic robot will take care of the simulacrums, but someone needs to stand guard in case a human tries to get through."

"I'm staying here and operating Arachne," Nadia said.

"Good," Madeline said.

"I can drive a Hummer," Jay said.

"Got those, too," L. M. said.

"Jay," Madeline said, "I need you to watch the building. You can stay here, but monitor the exterior. As long as everything's closed, there should be no possibility of a breach, but we need someone watching the outside just in case."

"Will do," Jay said.

"In that event," L. M. said, reaching for a cart filled with various items, "we need to equip you guys." She motioned to Daphne. "You, take a projectile gun and a spear gun, some handcuffs, and zip ties. Those work against simulacrums as well as humans. Nadia...."

"Spear gun," she said. "I'm SCUBA certified. I can use them."

L. M. nodded and walked over to Jay. "Jay, you need handcuffs," she looped one onto his belt, and held up a key, "key," she stuffed one in a pants pocket, "and zip ties." She put a bunch in his hand; he stuffed them in another pants pocket.

"No weapon?" Athena said with a wry smile.

"I'm good," Jay said.

Madeline held out an arm and turned around. "There are plenty of items around here Jay can pick up and use if he feels the need to. Those of us in the front, take a knife and let's go."

Madeline, Jean, Yolanda, Brittany, Sumita, and L. M. went through first. On his monitor, he saw L. M. lead them directly to a large cement building with a huge metal double door. On the way, they used their weapons to cut down the simulacrums in their path.

Immediately after they had gone, Nadia changed the position of the exit portal. Simulacrums attempting to run to where Madeline's team had appeared merely sprinted through air.

Nightmare trudged through next. Nadia changed the position of the exit portal again for Stacy to rumble through. She changed it again when Daphne walked over. After Daphne disappeared, Nadia turned to Jay. "I'm positioning the panic robot." She rolled it in front of the barrier, activated it, made sure the motion sensor was on, and came back to her laptop.

Jay kept an eye on multiple screens. The monitor on the outside of company headquarters showed nothing unusual. In contrast, the monitors on the Yeager estate displayed a lot of activity. Nightmare stomped on simulacrums, or picked them up and tossed them aside. STACY mowed them down. Madeline and her team ran them over with various vehicles. The combine shredded them. Jay counted more machines than there were members of Madeline's team; he guessed Yeager family members were driving some of the farm equipment. In addition, fireworks explosions caught and destroyed simulacrums which were closely gathered in clumps.

At the controls, Nadia continued to move the exit portal out of the way of simulacrums.

"Why not just shut it down until all the simulacrums are taken out?" Jay asked.

"Because activating it again would take time," Nadia said. "If we had an emergency, that's time we may not have."

The combined efforts of all the combatants steadily had an effect; the number of active simulacrums visibly declined. Still, Jay reckoned there had to be at least a few hundred left. Two of the farm machines were herding simulacrums; they came together in a clump, made a sudden right turn, and disappeared.

Nadia gasped. "They're inside Arachne! They got in before I could change the exit portal."

"Can you change it now?"

"Yes, but...."

Jay turned to the monitor. Simulacrums were being ejected out of the relocated portal. Jay saw ammo spheres.

"Daphne needs help," Nadia said, taking her spear gun. "You stay here."

"But what if...?" He called after her, but she passed the panic robot—which shot out light beams—and disappeared.

Jay turned to the monitors wondering what to do. Seconds passed. Nothing more came out of the exit portal. Nothing came in to the cave complex. He looked around. The cart had no more projectile guns, no "weed killers." More had to be in the back. He rushed away to the workshop stations to find one.

Arachne screamed.

Jay halted. No doubt it was Arachne. No doubt it had screamed.

He heard the panic robot wildly shooting off its beams. Although a partition blocked Jay's view of the lower part of Arachne, and of the control station, he heard footsteps on the stone floor. His first thought was to call Nadia's and Daphne's names, but, on second thought, what if it was an intruder?

He had to get a weapon. If it was Nadia or Daphne or one of the others, fine. Otherwise, he intended to defend himself and Arachne.

Chapter 13

Jay hurried to a weapons locker. He and L. M. had the security codes for all the lockers. After opening it, he found, to his relief, one of the projectile guns. He checked it over and found the mechanism easy to understand. After releasing the safety, he held it firmly and crept in the direction of Arachne.

He peered around the partition, hoping to see Nadia or Daphne, or both, but instead, he saw a man bending over Stephanie's laptop, inserting a memory card and downloading data. Stepping carefully, and he hoped, noiselessly, he got close enough to see the monitor overlooking the Yeager estate. Just outside the portal he saw a group of simulacrums surrounding Nadia and Daphne. They lay on the ground, unmoving.

He raised the gun. "If those women are dead, so are you."

The man started and turned around.

Jay straightened. "Don! I should have known."

He laughed nervously. "You aren't going to use that, are you, Jay?"

Jay's aim remained steady. "Try me."

Don took a breath. "They aren't dead. I used an advanced taser and had the simulacrums drag them out. It took a bunch of simulacrums to hold them so I could use the taser."

"You're a real brave man," Jay said sarcastically, thinking that the taser must have caused Arachne to scream.

"Would you have preferred that I shoot them?"

"You know the answer to that." Jay looked at Don steadily. "Well, now it all comes together. You were the one who tampered with my medication."

"You recovered."

"And that angel investor? Charles."

"Yes, but I can explain."

"And that corporate suite at the ballpark? Also courtesy of Charles."

"True. As I said, I can explain."

"Did you tamper with the vault at the museum, too?"

Don sighed.

"I'll take that as a 'yes.' And the job referral to Madeline? Was that Charles, too?"

"No, I never had contact with him until after you came to work here."

"Huh. Convenient."

"He gave me the money I needed to start my own business. No one was ever hurt."

"Your definition of 'hurt' differs from mine. Having my medication withdrawn fits my definition of 'harm.'"

"Well, then, I'm sorry."

"You realize, don't you, that I can kill you where you stand, deposit your body in a snowbank in Antarctica, and no one would ever know."

"You wouldn't do that, Jay."

"No, but Charles could if he had this device, did that ever occur to you?"

"Charles just wants it as a status symbol."

"Really? I never took you for someone who falls for a smooth lie, Don."

He spread his hands. "Jay, this is just a game to him. He wants to win, that's all. He wants his prize. He has enough money to pay for it. You know he's never been in trouble with the law."

"That anyone could prove, that is."

"Jay, if I didn't know you better, I'd say you're off your medication again. People don't like Charles because he's got a lot of money and isn't shy about throwing it around, that's all. You and the others here have adopted a siege mentality that's out of touch. Can't you see that?"

"And you, Don, have fallen hook, line, and sinker for Charles's story."

Don took a step forward. "Jay, why not drop the weapon and come with me? I can give you a good job at a good salary. You don't belong here."

"Says who?"

He waved his hand toward Jay. "Have you checked a mirror lately? You look just like them. You're only part of the machinery now. I hardly recognize you."

"I could say the same about you. Except that you sold your soul and I got mine back."

Don let out a heavy sigh. "Look, Jay, I'm taking this memory card..." he removed it from the laptop, "...and leaving."

Jay flipped the switch to the "ready" position. "And, I, Don, am going to shoot you."

Don shook his head. "No, you're not." He turned and began to walk toward Arachne.

Jay shot him in the back.

Don went down, breath knocked out of him. Jay dropped the gun, ran over, pulled Don's hands behind his back, and handcuffed him. Then he turned him over and put a knee on Don's stomach. He raised a fist, intending to beat the bloody hell out of him, but saw real fear in Don's face and stopped.

He dragged Don to his feet. "Get up." He pushed him underneath Athena's scanner.

"What is this? A disintegration chamber?"

"I wish." He worked the controls. In addition to the memory card, Don had a transmitter. Jay cleaned the memory card and deactivated the transmitter. When finished, he fished in Don's pockets and brought out a smartphone. Taking it apart, he said, "Oh, look, spying devices." He faced Don for a moment. "We'll just take those out and return this phone to factory settings." Once that was accomplished, he put the phone and devices back in Don's pocket.

Walking over to Nadia's laptop, he turned the satellite view on Las Vegas. Finding an alley behind a restaurant near the main strip, he set the coordinates there. Arachne responded in standard fashion. He walked over, grabbed Don, and pushed him toward Arachne.

"Where are we going?"

"You'll see. Wait, just a minute." He used a zip tie to secure Don to a post and stopped at his booth to put on a mask, helmet, and goggles.

When he emerged and took off the zip tie, Don shook his head. "I suppose you think you're some sort of hero."

"No, I think *you're* some sort of asshole. Come on."

Once they emerged, Jay used another zip tie to secure the handcuffs to a dumpster. He walked around and faced Don. "You're in Las Vegas. Seeing people handcuffed is everyday business here. Someone will come along eventually. You can use your cell phone to call Charles to pick you up, *if* you can remember his number. Or, since your wallet's in your pocket, charge a ticket back home. So long, Don." He took a step toward the portal and stopped. "If you ever see me again, I suggest you pretend not to know me; I definitely will deny ever knowing you." He walked back into the portal.

When he came out, the panic robot greeted him with a light show. As he took off his helmet, goggles, and mask, his cell phone rang. "Jay, Jay, are you there?" Madeline said.

"Yes, I'm here. Sorry for the delay. I was taking out the garbage."

"What?"

"Metaphorically speaking. I'll explain later."

"Can you open up Arachne? Do you know how to use it?"

"Yes, and yes. I'll have you here in no time."

Madeline, Jean, Yolanda, and L. M. came through first. Brittany came next, guiding Nadia; Sumita appeared right behind them, arm around Daphne. When they cleared Arachne, STACY began to rumble through, followed by Nightmare.

"Are you two all right?" Jay called.

"Just stunned." Nadia took a tall chair and sank into it.

Daphne nodded. "We were overwhelmed. We couldn't fight off a dozen simulacrums at once."

Yolanda said, "Well, you gave it a good try."

Madeline turned to Jay. "Nadia and Daphne said there was a human with a taser. Did he get in here?"

"Yes, it was Don."

Madeline took a step back as if someone had pushed her. "Don?"

L. M. turned around. "Where'd you put him?"

"I handcuffed him to a dumpster in the back of a restaurant in Vegas."

"Good for you!" Yolanda said.

Madeline sighed. "Pity. He used to be a nice guy."

"'Used to be' is right," Jay agreed.

"Sorry to have lost him," L. M. said. "I would have loved to interrogate him."

Yolanda crossed her arms in front of her. "Why? He'd just lie."

L. M. grinned. "There are ways to get a lying perp to give you what you need."

"We have everything we need to know from him," Madeline said.

Meanwhile, Athena and Terry walked up to the control center.

Jay took a deep breath. "There's something else." When they all turned to him, he said, "When Nadia and Daphne didn't appear from Arachne, I went back and got a gun. By the time I came back, Don was in here and he put a memory card in Stephanie's laptop."

Immediately, Nadia lunged toward the laptop and consulted it.

After the "what!" exclamations died down, Jay pointed to Athena's scanner. "I put him under the scanner. I cleaned the memory card and deactivated the transmitters. I also returned his smartphone to factory settings, just for good measure."

"Where's the memory card?" Athena asked.

"I put it back in his pocket. I didn't want him, or Charles, by extension, to accuse us of theft."

"Theft?" Athena said. "At the least, we could charge him, and Charles, with industrial espionage, trespassing, and assault."

"Yeah, but Jay still did the right thing," L. M. said.

Nadia turned to Madeline and nodded. "He downloaded what we think he did."

"Without the memory card, we can't confirm that he has nothing," Athena said.

"Oh, Charles will let us know that soon enough," Yolanda said.

Madeline held up a hand for silence. "All right, we need to think this through." She turned to Terry. "Terry, the Yeagers still need you to supervise cleaning up the simulacrums."

Nadia dialed Arachne. Terry nodded, rolled the panic robot away, and walked back to Arachne's entrance. "But let me know how this turns out," she said over her shoulder.

"We're calling a company meeting," Madeline said. "We'll bring you back when we're ready." She leaned over to Nadia. "Start calling everyone. Tell them it should only be a few hours and then they can all go back to their vacations."

"I can help call," Jay said.

"No, I need more information from you first," Madeline said. "Replay the cave complex monitor from when Don came in."

Jay used Stephanie's laptop and replayed the recording.

"That sonuvabitch," Athena said in a low voice.

L. M. pointed to the screen. "That's why we can't turn Don, or Charles, in. If we take this to court, Arachne becomes public information."

"And they know it," Yolanda added.

By this time, the vacationing company employees started coming through Arachne.

Madeline turned to L. M. "About how many simulacrums do we still have corralled over at the estate?"

"Whole ones? Oh, maybe 20 or 30."

Madeline turned to Nadia. "Get the GPS coordinates of Charles's office at his company headquarters."

"You're going to put the simulacrums there?" Yolanda smiled. "I'm all for it!"

"Simulacrums?" Vivian had just walked around the barrier.

Madeline turned to her. "Vivian, I need my killer outfit. Let's go." After putting a hand on Vivian's back, she looked at Athena. "I'll need a spy camera, too."

"You're going to bait the bear in his den?" Yolanda said. "About time!"

Stephanie, Ginnie Mae, Zoe, and Irene gathered around the control console.

Irene peered at the laptop screens. "Have you been having fun without us?"

Daphne, seated in a tall chair similar to Nadia's, had just accepted a cup of coffee from Sumita. "If you can call getting tased fun."

Sumita walked over and gave another cup of coffee to Nadia.

"Tased?" Stephanie queried.

"Showdown at the Yeager estate," L. M. said, "with simulacrums. We mowed 'em down, and now we're dealing with the aftermath."

"What aftermath?" Jean said. "Don't we have this pretty much wrapped up?"

L. M. sighed. "Hell, no." She turned to Jay. "Give me a long satellite view of the estate and the surroundings." When Jay complied, she added, "Look at that. Simulacrum pieces everywhere. Look at the roads. Gridlock from the county seat all the way to the estate."

"What are all those people doing there?" Irene asked.

"We had Stacy out, Nightmare out, all the big farm equipment out, and using fireworks to blow up the simulacrums. People came from miles around to see what the commotion was. The switchboard lit up and Cousin Andy is hard pressed taking all the calls."

"Complaints?" Jean asked.

"Nothing but. 'Why didn't you advertise this in advance?' 'I didn't see anything on the website about tickets.' 'I've been coming to your events for years and I'm very annoyed that you didn't offer me premium seats,' and so forth."

Athena burst out into laughter.

"You think it's funny, but it's a PR disaster," L. M. said. "Aunt Thelma and Uncle Ned say we have to plan an extra special New Year's extravaganza to make up for it."

"To put it in perspective," Brittany said, "I'd rather deal with this sort of problem than with Charles any day."

"You're right." Nadia reached over and put a hand on Athena's shoulder. "Come on, Madeline will be back any minute."

Athena raised her head and took a breath. "Sorry, I couldn't help it." She walked back to her workshop, chuckling to herself.

While waiting for Madeline, Nadia put a portal on the Yeager estate so that Terry could bring the simulacrums through. Jay braced himself for trouble, but they seemed docile enough with Terry around.

"I've interrupted the signal to their handlers," Terry explained.

Meanwhile, the others explained what happened with Don for Ginnie Mae, Irene, Stephanie, and Zoe. Jay replayed the recording.

Stephanie turned to Nadia and exchanged a look.

"Yes, he got it," Nadia said.

The door above the ramp opened. Madeline walked in. She looked sharp in a navy blue pantsuit, which could have been a military uniform except for the lack of insignia. She wore no hat, carried no purse.

Athena met her at the base of the walkway, holding out a hand. "Is this what you wanted?"

Madeline nodded. She grasped a lapel pin and put it on.

"I have Charles's office suite," Nadia said.

"Good. Put the simulacrums in the lobby, first."

Nadia dialed Arachne; Terry herded the simulacrums inside, returning after a few moments. "That'll keep Charles's security crew busy."

Jay pointed to the screen on Stephanie's laptop, showing a satellite view of Charles's headquarters. "You can see the simulacrums through the glass."

Madeline nodded. "Now let's see if Nadia can pick up the lapel camera."

Nadia made some adjustments on the screen. On one of the screen windows, they saw everyone standing in front of Madeline.

Madeline straightened her suit. "Now, dial Charles's office suite."

"Do you think he's there?" Jean asked.

"He's there," Madeline said. "Make sure you record everything."

"Will do," Nadia said.

"Be careful," Jean said. "Charles may be expecting you to walk into his trap."

"No, he'll be walking into mine," Madeline strolled around the barrier and stopped in front of Arachne.

By this time, the others had chairs at the control console. Stephanie and Nadia sat behind their respective laptops. Jay sat between them. The others pushed chairs near them to get a clear view of the screen.

Nadia dialed up Arachne. "Go, Madeline, and good luck."

The view from Madeline's lapel pin disappeared when she walked into Arachne. When the screen became active again, they saw an office with floor-to-ceiling windows on two sides. It brightened further when Madeline turned on the lights. As far as they could see, she was the only one there. She walked past the bookcases, the couches around the low table, and the mini-kitchen, to behind a polished mahogany desk filled with the latest communications equipment. She sat in the high-backed, leather-upholstered chair behind the desk, facing a laptop with a large screen showing Charles's company logo as the wallpaper.

The main door opened and Charles walked in. He spotted Madeline and smiled. "Miss Chang," he said pleasantly. He walked to the desk and stood in front of it.

Madeline remained seated. "Mr. Vance."

He smiled. "To what do I owe the pleasure?"

"Just delivering a gift."

"The simulacrums in the lobby? Technically, not a gift, since I own them."

"Technically, a gift," Madeline said evenly, "since *I* own them."

He shifted his weight, but his smile never dimmed. "Previous owner."

"Current owner. You see, I purchased the license, and all the stock, from your manufacturer. I allowed them to deliver the ones you ordered, but I was the owner of record at that time."

"Indeed."

"Though if I had known what you had planned to use them for, I might have interrupted that delivery."

"Unexpected events are disconcerting, aren't they?" He put his hands behind his back, and lowered his head, as if thinking. "Very well, you own the license, but I still own the rights."

She folded her hands on the table. "I'm in a much more favorable situation now than I was at the time you made the original purchase of rights. The difference between us is that my company is small enough that I sign off on everything that happens in my company. With such large holdings, you delegate much of your negotiating authority to lieutenants. One of them found my offer of a rights purchase very attractive indeed."

He grinned and nodded. "I shall have to fire him."

"Oh, I don't think you'll do that. In fact, I think you'll give him a bonus, don't you?"

158 Joan Marie Verba

He chuckled and shook his head. "You play a very entertaining game of chess."

She smiled. "You have no idea."

He held up a finger. "I think I do. You're right, it was never about the simulacrums. Means to an end."

"Arachne."

"Arachne." He paced in front of his desk. "Of course, you would never sell the rights or license to that. Might fall into the wrong hands."

"Such as yours," she said confidently.

He stopped pacing and spread his hands. "Your opinion." He held up a finger again. "And, it's too big to move." He tapped his lips with a finger. "What to do? What to do?"

"Let me cut to the chase," Madeline said. "Your agent failed to get the plans to Arachne."

He faced her. "You think so?"

"I know so."

He leaned toward her. "Are you certain?"

"Absolutely."

He sidled up to the chair and waved toward the laptop. "May I?"

She stood. "Your laptop."

He sat and cleared the screen. A file came into view. As Charles continued to type or mouse over, he said, "I had a talk with my agent. Of course, you, or rather, your lieutenant, as you put it, wiped the memory card clean and disabled the transmitter. However, what your lieutenant did not seem to realize was that the memory card also had a transmitter. As soon as it connected to the laptop, and before your lieutenant showed up, it retrieved and sent all the information it gathered, right...here." He leaned back and gave Madeline room to examine the screen more closely.

She did.

In the cave complex, Nadia and Stephanie leaned toward Stephanie's laptop screen and looked over the plans.

"Well?" Athena demanded. "Are those the plans for Arachne?"

Stephanie and Nadia looked at each other, and then turned back to look at L. M.

"Bingo!" L. M. said.

Athena turned to L. M. "Get a grip! This is serious!"

"Relax," L. M. said. "She still has an ace up her sleeve."

Terry moved closer to the screen and pointed to a section of the plans. "Athena, look at that."

Athena scrutinized the readout. "Wait a minute... Arachne doesn't have..." She turned to Stephanie. "They're fake!"

Stephanie grinned. "Of course they are."

"You might have said something."

"Be fair, Athena," Brittany said. "Madeline, L. M., Stephanie, and Nadia couldn't be sure when Charles's agents would show up or which one of us that agent would talk to. Because we didn't know, we could look genuinely alarmed when the agent took the bait."

Athena nodded. "Okay, that makes sense. I'm not happy about it, but it makes sense."

Meanwhile, Madeline flipped from screen to screen on Charles's laptop, while Charles looked on triumphantly.

Eventually, Madeline straightened up and turned to Charles wordlessly.

"Oh, I'll still let you do your little humanitarian operation," Charles said. "The public loves it, and I must say it's quite entertaining."

"Not to mention useful," Madeline said, "as with your granddaughter?"

For the first time, Charles assumed a serious expression. "Yes, unfortunately, there are still events beyond my control. But with my own device, I won't have to depend on intermediaries when that happens."

"I wouldn't count on that," Madeline said.

Charles raised an eyebrow. "Don't worry. I won't let on to what you have, and you won't let on to what I have, or we'll both be exposed."

"Just what are you plans for it?" Madeline asked. "Other than to deal with unexpected events, that is."

"Anything I want, that's the point, isn't it?" Charles smiled. "The possibilities are limitless."

"I can imagine," Madeline said.

"Balance of power," Charles said.

"I call it something else."

"Doubtless you do." He frowned slightly. "Now, I'm afraid, our interview is over. I presume you know the way out."

Madeline picked up her smartphone. Jay answered the call.

"Put the portal behind me," Madeline said.

Within seconds, Madeline stepped back and Charles's office disappeared from the screen.

Chapter 14

When Madeline stepped out of the portal, Athena rushed up to her. "Congratulations. Your plan worked. But I still have some questions."

Madeline nodded. "Let's gather in the conference room."

When they were assembled, Madeline in her chair, Athena said, "I presume Charles is going to build something from those plans that looks like Arachne, but what's he going to build?"

"A very large musical instrument, which will play one tune." L. M. took the toothpick out of her mouth and waved it like a baton as she sang the first lines of "One Way or Another." She replaced the toothpick and smiled.

Madeline turned to her, but did not demand she lose the toothpick. The others chuckled.

Athena turned back to Madeline. "Wait a minute. There's more in Stephanie's laptop than the supposed plans to Arachne. There's the activation protocol, the Symphony Robotics software that now holds all of our location data, and a bunch of other proprietary material."

Nadia shook her head. "He didn't get those, either."

"Well, he got something!" Athena said.

Nadia smiled. "When you use a computer, you rely on preprogrammed commands. The protocol that copies files. The protocol that erases files. And so forth. Those are the same for almost every computer. That's what computer data thieves take advantage of. They give those commands, and the computer automatically uploads or downloads the information."

Athena spread her hands. "Yeah. That's presumably how Charles got the information."

Nadia shook her head. "I reprogrammed my and Stephanie's laptop. Those standard commands won't work on our computers— at least, they won't work the way they do on yours. Instead, anything that activates those commands is directed to an isolated section of memory that has all sorts of lovely false information. The actual working data is completely untouched, and behind a very strong firewall."

Stephanie turned to Athena. "Even if someone figured it out—and I doubt they would—the plans to Arachne are not only not on my computer, they aren't anywhere in the building."

"What did you do, put them in a safe deposit box somewhere?" Athena asked.

"They're on the moon," Madeline said.

Athena turned to her.

"One very lonely night, after Zoe had finished her maintenance work, Stephanie, Jean, and I directed Arachne to the moon. Jean had astronaut training in the Air Force; she put on the spacesuit and buried a box containing the datacard in a crater."

"Works for me!" Jay exclaimed.

Madeline, Stephanie, and Jean smiled.

"One thing wrong with that," Athena said. "We need Arachne to get to the moon, but we'd need the plans if we ever had to rebuild Arachne. How would we get the plans?"

Madeline smiled. "We also buried a set on the company's private island."

"That works," Athena said.

"Anything else?" Madeline looked around the table.

"Question?" Jay asked.

Madeline turned to him. "Of course."

"The Yeagers...I presume they can tell a simulacrum from a human?"

"Oh, yeah, they know," L. M. said.

"They've been helpful with several of our projects," Madeline said. "By the way, anyone have any trouble getting away from family to use Arachne?"

"I just said I was going for a walk," Ginnie Mae said.

"Me, too," Irene said.

"Ever since I told my family that the gravy train has left the station," Vivian said, "they're happy to see me go out for a while."

"Just as long as they didn't see you disappear." Madeline pushed back her chair. "Now we can all go back to our vacations."

* * *

Those at the residence for winter break still felt the need to keep busy, so they pitched in to help the Yeagers. Terry returned to supervising the cleanup of the simulacrums. L. M.'s Uncle Ned asked her if she could bring Nightmare for the New Year's Eve show. Terry replied that the company's machinery was proprietary, but volunteered to draw up plans for and supervise construction of a large dinosaur robot frame, which they seemed to be equally happy with. Similarly, Athena refused to bring STACY back for display, but offered to give them directions on how to customize a pickup truck to make an impressive-looking vehicle. Nadia made improvements to their ticketing system and website. Brittany came up with recipes for additional offerings they could add to their snack menu. Jay helped Cousin Andy at the switchboard. Sumita and Jean remained at company headquarters, to facilitate the others going back and forth.

On the evening of the 31st, L. M. led them to a berm where they could get a good view of the show and the fireworks. They spread out blankets and opened folding chairs. Most of the spectators filled the reviewing stands on the other side of the field.

The show consisted of a drama featuring dinosaur vs. pickup truck, which the crowd loved, followed by a concert, and topped off by fireworks at midnight. After the fireworks, they made their farewells to the Yeagers, and returned to the cave complex, where Athena, who watched the show on the satellite monitor, waited for them.

On New Year's Day, the rest of the company employees trickled back. "Need to help them bring in their Christmas loot," L. M. said at their shared breakfast in Sumita and Brittany's apartment.

Brittany, Jean, Athena, and Jay took turns picking up fellow employees at the airport and driving them back to the residence. They parked their cars in the outdoor lot to unload, saving them from hauling the bags an extra floor.

As Jay helped Stephanie with her bags, he said, "I don't think you saw that part of the security feed yet, but Arachne screamed when Don tased Daphne and Nadia."

Stephanie pulled the handle of her roller bag. "Screamed?"

Jay nodded. "I'm sure it was Arachne."

Stephanie took a long breath. "Another aspect of Arachne I can't yet account for, I guess."

There was an elevator inside; they took it.

"Another thing. When L. M. took me through Arachne after Thanksgiving, I heard Arachne singing. She only heard music. I heard it sing again when I left Don in Vegas."

Stephanie shook her head when the elevator door opened. "I don't know, Jay. Did L. M. say anything?"

"She said I should ask Sumita. When I did at breakfast this morning, L. M. added Arachne likes me."

Stephanie chuckled as she opened her apartment door. "She would."

"Sumita said that because I have some brain damage, perhaps my brain was interpreting Arachne's sound waves differently."

"That's as good an explanation as any, I guess."

Just before lunch, they assembled in the parking lot waiting for Jean to bring back Madeline, and Brittany to bring back Irene.

"Why two drivers?" Jay asked.

Sumita turned to him. "Brittany has to drive Irene's grandmother to the assisted living facility first. They went to and from California together."

Brittany and Irene arrived as Jean unloaded Madeline's bags. When Irene came out of the car, carrying a backpack, she strode directly to Stephanie. "The television news at the airport said that a communications satellite is falling to Earth today in the Gulf of California. Is that close enough for us to see it?"

Vivian looked up, shading her eyes. "Is that it?"

Jay tilted his head upward and saw what appeared to be a star in the clear blue daytime sky.

Madeline, who had a suitcase in hand, dropped it. "Stephanie, we need to get inside and check this, now."

They all hurried into company headquarters and rushed into the cave complex. As Stephanie and Nadia turned on their computers, Madeline asked Irene, "Did they say what company the satellite belonged to?"

"Gigantic Communications."

"One of Charles's subsidiaries," Yolanda said.

Nadia focused in on it. "It's breaking apart as it falls. The pieces are spreading out."

Stephanie turned from her screen to Nadia's and back. "Those little pieces won't cause much damage, if they reach Earth at all. It's that central piece...."

Athena pointed at the screen. "Wait a minute. That's exhaust coming from that core piece. It's being guided."

Stephanie swung around. "It's being guided to us."

"Charles wouldn't be stupid enough to kill us all, would he?" Jean asked.

"He probably thinks we're all either gone or in the residence," Yolanda said. "It's a holiday, after all."

"Just our luck," Athena said. "This is the *only* thing with enough energy to destroy this structure."

"Will it make a crater?" Ginnie Mae asked.

Stephanie shook her head. "Not large enough to make much of one." She pointed to the ceiling. "It will probably punch through about there and destroy everything down here."

"Like a guided missile," Athena added.

"He's after Arachne." Madeline turned to Stephanie and Nadia. "Now that he thinks he has his own, he wants to get rid of ours. Can you put a portal under it and direct it to the Gulf of California?"

They nodded.

Their computers erupted into a geyser of sparks. Both women jumped back.

Athena crossed her arms and turned to Jay. "It seems your former friend Don left a present when he was here."

"It didn't show on the monitor recordings," Stephanie said.

"The download device must have left behind something on remote control to short out the system," Nadia said.

"That's irrelevant now," Daphne said. "The question is, what are our alternatives?"

"You do have backup computers with duplicates of all your data?" Athena asked.

"Yes," Nadia said, "but we couldn't get them activated and aligned in time."

"How long do we have?" Madeline said.

"Five, ten minutes, maybe," Stephanie said.

"Time for me to save our butts again." L. M. turned to Jay. "*Your* computer should be just fine. Get me the GPS coordinates."

Jay sprinted to his desk. L. M. ran behind. The others hurried after them.

Stephanie took a chair and sat next to Jay. "I need to get in on this."

Jay nodded. "Okay, locked on to the satellite."

"I'll take that," Stephanie said. "You bring up a second screen with a clear area over the Gulf of California."

"Got it," Jay said.

Stephanie shook her head. "This is going to be tricky. I have to predict a point below it that it will fall into, *and* I have to align that portal horizontally instead of vertically." She used the computer to make some calculations, and sent the orientation coordinates to Jay's screen with the GPS numbers.

Jay pointed to the combined series of numbers on his screen and turned to L. M. "Those are your destination coordinates."

L. M. sang a crescendo. "Aah–aah-aah-aah-aah-aah–aah."

Stephanie turned to L. M. and pointed to another window on the screen. "Those are your origin coordinates."

L. M. sang again. When finished, she said, "Got it." She ran to Arachne.

"Need any help?" Stephanie called after her.

"No," she called as she ran.

Madeline waved to the others. "We have to get to the shelter underneath the residence. There's no guarantee that this place won't be hit."

"But I don't want to leave Stephanie, Jay, and L. M. here alone," Irene protested.

"None of us do," Yolanda said. "But we have to go. Hopefully we'll be back together soon."

Madeline ushered them out. "Good luck." She turned to Terry as they walked to the entrance to the tunnel to the residence. "Can you call the Santanas and tell them to take cover?"

"They set the automatic alarms and took their staff and the horses to a New Year's horse fair," Terry said. "They won't be back until the 6th."

Meanwhile, Jay added a monitor window to his screen, showing the cave complex. L. M. stopped in front of Arachne. She remained quiet until she was breathing normally again.

Stephanie turned on the intercom. "There's no time to lose. That core piece is coming fast."

L. M. took a deep breath and began to sing. Arachne lit up and sang back.

Stephanie waved at the screen. "She's doing it. It's working."

They turned to the monitors. The core piece disappeared from Stephanie's window...and reappeared in Jay's window, slamming into the Gulf of California.

Jay leaned toward the intercom. "Butts saved, L. M." Then he texted Madeline's phone. "All clear."

When L. M. came back to the main floor, she was greeted with hugs and back pats from her returned colleagues. Jay accessed the cable news and put the broadcast on the large screen. The press had, all along, been expecting the satellite to drop into the Gulf of California and reported such, with pictures.

"Charles knows he's failed." Jean turned to Madeline.

Yolanda also turned to Madeline. "He crossed a line this time, Madeline."

Madeline took a long breath and nodded.

"Revenge?" Brittany said. "Not sure I'd recommend that. Tends to backfire."

"We can't do nothing," Athena insisted.

"I didn't say do nothing," Brittany said. "But we need to consider any move against Charles very carefully."

"I always do," Madeline said.

Stephanie stood and motioned to Nadia. "While you're plotting against Charles, Nadia and I will get the backup computers from the vault and set them up."

"And I," Athena said, "will sweep the cave complex to be sure that Jay's ex-friend hasn't left us any other surprises."

"I'll help," Terry said, and followed.

"Me, too," Ginnie Mae said, and scrambled after them.

Madeline took Stephanie's seat next to Jay. "When I was searching for an island to purchase or claim for the company, I came across a lot of candidates." She took command of Jay's computer.

"You're going to strand him on an island?" Jean asked.

Madeline kept her eyes on the screen as images and maps materialized. "That's the idea."

"How do you know he'll survive?" Brittany asked.

"We'll give him a satellite phone," Madeline said.

Jay turned to Brittany. "We're going to be making a point."

"Not that I disapprove, but isn't that kidnapping?" Jean asked.

Jay turned around to her. "No, that's just giving him a 2500-mile lift."

"How's he going to have us arrested without telling the authorities about Arachne?" L. M. said. "Ain't going to happen."

Madeline pointed to the screen. "That one. It's close enough that he can call one of his subsidiaries to send him a helicopter, and far enough away so that he's going to be uncomfortable for a while."

Jay held up a hand. "Madeline, I want to volunteer to take Charles through Arachne."

"You're not going to beat him to a pulp?"

"You saw the monitor replay. Don's bones are still intact."

Brittany rubbed her chin thoughtfully. "There's something to be said about that, Madeline. Sending Jay—or any one of us—instead of doing it yourself reinforces the message that you can't be bothered with him anymore."

L. M. grinned. "Yeah."

Madeline turned from Brittany to L. M. to Jay. "All right, Jay, the job's yours."

Chapter 15

Within the hour, Nadia and Stephanie had their backup computers activated and running. Athena, Terry, and Ginnie Mae confirmed there were no further unauthorized devices in the cave complex—though, since Jay had touched Don, Athena scanned him just to be sure nothing had been left on Jay. Terry brought over a simulacrum—she had started making them again, and this time she had an abundance of spare parts from the Yeagers.

"I can control it from here," Terry explained. "I'll see and hear everything it does."

"I'm still not sure I need it," Jay said.

"You will," L. M. said. "Charles isn't going to go with you without a struggle, and the simulacrum can do the heavy lifting."

Jay nodded. "Now that you mention it, I guess we can't be sure Charles won't come up with something unexpected."

Athena beckoned to him. "Bend down, I want to add a button to your collar."

Jay still wore the shirt, jeans, and walking shoes and socks that he had put on that morning. Athena attached the camera to his shirt. When he straightened, Athena handed him a slender satellite phone. "It's expendable. I made sure it's at factory settings. All he can do with it is make phone calls." Jay put it in a jeans pocket.

L. M. handed him sunglasses. "Wear these, too. It'll make you look more intimidating."

Jay put them on and nodded. They fit well, and he could see everything clearly.

L. M. gave him handcuffs and a key. "Need zip ties?"

He took them. "No, these'll do."

Irene walked up and handed him a brown paper lunch bag. "Here."

Jay opened it and looked inside. He saw a large covered container of coffee, and a transparent food container holding a sandwich and a large pickle, split in two.

"Ham and cheese sandwich on rye, in case he gets hungry," Irene explained.

Athena groaned. Some of the other women chuckled.

"Take it," L. M. said. "Food is always good as leverage."

Jay closed the bag and folded the top.

Nadia leaned in his direction. "If you're ready, you can go through Arachne to Charles's office, and then to the island."

"We have a satellite view of the island and your button camera is working," Stephanie added.

"Good luck; you're going to need it," L. M. said.

Jay smiled and walked to Arachne. The simulacrum followed. Once he stepped inside, he could see the interior of Charles's office. He inched right up to the exit portal, but did not walk in.

Charles sat behind his desk, facing a knot of men standing in front of him—backs to Jay. The men wore lab coats.

"I don't want hear your excuses," Charles said firmly. "You told me you could guide that satellite right to that building with pinpoint precision, and you failed."

"We could try again," one of the men said feebly.

"There was only one try!" Charles insisted. "Now, we'll be watched even more closely. No, you're not going to try it again. Get back to work on that device. If you don't have that running the way it's supposed to, I'll see that none of you are able to get any job higher than a janitor. Go!"

The men hurried out.

When the door was shut, Charles left his desk and walked to the kitchen area. He put a thick glass on the counter and reached for ice tongs.

Jay pushed the simulacrum ahead of him. It moved quickly and quietly toward Charles and grabbed him by the arm as he was putting ice in the glass.

Charles dropped the tongs and turned. "What the...? Who let this thing in here?"

Jay had stepped out by this time, stopping one pace in front of Charles. "I did."

He turned to Jay. "Who the hell are you?"

Jay tilted his sunglasses so that Charles could see his eyes. "I'm the one on the high ground, remember?" Jay let go of the eyeglasses again.

"What do you want?"

"We're going for a walk." Jay turned.

The simulacrum followed, dragging Charles. He tried to struggle free, but was held fast. Once he was within Arachne, he stopped struggling and looked around.

"Savor it," Jay said. "You'll never get a view from yours." He could see the island through the exit portal, and in the next moment, strode out, Charles and the simulacrum at his heels.

At once, Jay felt a warm sea breeze and smelled the refreshing tang of salt air. The place had plenty of plants; he chose one with a thick stem and clamped one ring of the handcuffs around it. When the simulacrum brought Charles over, he grasped Charles's wrist and secured the other ring around it. When he stepped back, the simulacrum let Charles go.

"What's the point of all this?" Charles demanded.

"The point is, we can find you at any time and take you wherever we want to take you."

Charles smiled. "That ability will not be unique to you for long."

"Don't count on it. Meanwhile, I want you to think, and think hard, that next time we could put you in some place a little less pleasant—or so compromising that you'd have to hire ten PR firms to get your reputation back."

Charles pulled on the handcuffs. The plant held him fast. "Maybe I can't reach you, but there are the Yeagers."

"I wouldn't mess with them if I were you. Your datamining subsidiaries may have found out who they are and how much they make, but I've been there. I've seen their wall of photos. They've given tours to the governor, both senators, the U. S. attorney general, and oh, have I mentioned one of their relatives is the Secretary of the Navy?"

Charles scowled.

"Something else to consider. You said it yourself. People love the 'Emergency Choristers.' They think the Yeagers are the cream of the crop. You're not only going to keep quiet about Arachne because it would expose your ambitions; you'll keep quiet about it because you know that if it came to a public battle of reputations, we'd win hands down."

"There won't be any public confrontations. You forget that I'll soon have my own device, and then I can do what I want, when I want to, and no one will need to know about it, either."

"How many times do we have to tell you that you don't have the plans to Arachne?"

"My experts say otherwise."

"Well, you'll see soon enough."

"Let's drop the pretense, shall we? You're desperate because I have the plans, so you're trying to deter me from using them by telling me I don't actually have them."

Jay took a deep breath. "Suit yourself." He fished into his pocket.

"You're not going to just leave me here, are you?"

Jay pulled out the satellite phone. "You know we won't." He extended the phone to Charles. "Here. You can call someone to pick you up."

He took it with his free hand and looked at it. "How do I know it'll work?"

Jay took it back and dialed a weather information line. He put it on speaker so Charles could hear it, then hung up the phone and stuffed it into one of Charles's suit pockets. After that, he extended the bag. "Here. It's a ham and cheese sandwich on rye, so you can have something to eat while waiting for your crew to show up."

Charles took the bag. "How do I know it's not poisoned?"

Jay sighed and grabbed the bag. "If that's how you feel, *I'll* have it for lunch, then."

Charles reached out. "All right, give it to me. I'll take it." When he had it in hand, he added, "You don't happen to have a brandy on you, do you?"

Jay looked skyward briefly. "I'm not a bartender." He turned to go, and then stopped. "Oh, I almost forgot." He took out the handcuff key and tucked it into Charles's shirt pocket. "You can let yourself loose once I'm gone. Bye." Without waiting for an answer, he hurried back into the portal. The simulacrum followed.

When he stepped into the cave complex, simulacrum in tow, he called, "Shut Arachne down, just in case."

"Already done," Stephanie called back.

Jay walked to the control console, where the others had gathered around the screens. Irene waved him over and pointed. "Look, he's eating the sandwich. He must have been hungry."

Jay took off the sunglasses and leaned forward for a better view. Charles had already freed himself and taken a bite out of the sandwich. From his expression, he seemed to be enjoying his meal.

"Gee, if I'd known he wanted a brandy, I would have sent along one of my souvenir liquor bottles," Athena said.

"Then he would have asked for a snifter, too," L. M. said.

"The man certainly has an ego," Brittany said. "He's so used to winning, to getting his own way, that he can't imagine failure."

Madeline put a hand on Jay's shoulder. "You did well, Jay. Thank you."

The first few weeks of the new year, Jay kept alert for any news from Charles, but there was none. As the days went on, he and the others became busy with company activities—which now included regularly going out to rescue someone. Immersed in his work, he gradually forgot all about Charles.

...until one day, when, after her usual choir practice, Irene came in from the cave complex, waving at Jay excitedly. "Jay, Jay, come and see!"

Jay made a quick check of the outside monitors and rose from his chair. "What is it?"

"Charles is activating his fake Arachne. Stephanie built something into the plans to let us know." She turned and hurried back the way she came.

"Wait...," Jay began, but she was gone. He set the phone system to voice mail and locked the outside doors before sprinting to the cave complex. Once he reached the cave floor, he joined Irene and the rest of the employees gathered around Arachne's control console.

L. M. turned to him, toothpick in mouth, and smiled. "The grand finale."

Jay looked at the screen. A window showed sort of a bar graph with lines going up and down. It reminded him of a sound monitor.

Stephanie pointed to it and turned it on. "It's powering up now."

"Pity we can't get a video," Athena said.

"If I had added video, he would have known the plans were fake," Stephanie said.

"It was easier to sneak in a sound transmitter," Nadia said, "since Arachne makes sounds."

"Can we hear if anyone near the fake is talking?" Jay asked.

"Yes," Stephanie said, "but so far it's been quiet, as if they're all holding their breaths." She turned to the monitor as the lines rose on the screen. "There it is." When she turned up the volume, they heard the tune for "One Way or Another."

"Yes, we got you, Charles!" Daphne exclaimed.

"Too bad he can't hear us," Athena said.

In the background, they could hear Charles's voice shouting expletives.

Jay turned to his colleagues. "I think his scientific staff will be out job hunting soon."

They all exchanged knowing looks as the fake continued to play the tune even louder, drowning out anything else Charles or his staff might be saying.

"Look," Irene said. "Arachne has lit up."

Stephanie smiled. "Arachne responds to any tune." She consulted her screen and added, "It hasn't opened a portal to anywhere, though: this particular song doesn't correspond to a code sequence."

"Arachne's celebrating," Terry said. "Let's celebrate, as well: choose your partners!" When Irene stepped toward her, she and Irene locked arms and circled each other in a country dance. The rest of them joined in as "One Way or Another" played in the background.